The 13th of Summer

Published by BooxAi
ISBN 978-965-577-959-2

The 13th of Summer

C.L. Pratt

Contents

Part One
The 13Th Of Summer

1. Betty	11
2. The Travelers	17
3. Before the Storm	21
4. Lloyd	25
5. Into the Storm	31
6. Back to the Farm	35
7. The Real Deal	39
8. Spread the Word	43
9. A Plan of Sorts	47
10. The Cemetery	51
11. The Bank	57
12. The Auction	63
13. A New Beginning	69

Part Two
Black Blizzard, White

14. The Hard Facts	75
15. November 11th, 1940	79
16. The Promise	83
17. The Blizzard	87
18. Christian and Willow	91
19. The Aftermath	97
20. At the End of the Road	103
21. The Silent Scream	109
22. After All is Said and Done	111

Part Three
East of summer

23. East of Summer	119
24. The Reunion	123
25. Home at Last	127

Part One

The 13Th Of Summer

Chapter 1

Betty

South Dakota was blowing away. Dirt was everywhere and on everything, and it took everything from everybody, their breath, their life. There were no exceptions. Brown, the color of dirt, brown, the color of life.

Etta slowly made her way across the dry, gritty yard, dust curling around her feet settling on her legs and dress. The sun beat down on her with a vengeance making the earth and Etta shimmer in the daylight as if they were mirages, like nothing was real. The earth, the buildings, the sky were all the same color, like old photos that were locked away from the ravages of time.

Etta was having another baby, a baby the Petersons could not afford. There were already six mouths to feed on a farm that was not producing anything. And Etta was about to give birth again.

Betty, a slight girl with blonde hair and dark brown eyes, stood behind a rickety screen door, watching her mother move slowly toward the house. Etta, heavy with child, walked slowly, deliberately with every step. The grasshoppers would jump out of her way, but there were so many everything was defenseless, against the marauding hoard that ate with a vengeance. It was useless to try to step around them.

The hot, dry August world had been the same on the South Dakota prairie for a long time and seemed to run on forever, unbroken by any hint of humanity. The next farm stood a quarter of a mile down the road from the Peterson place. It was the Foley's homestead and they were desperate like so many of the South Dakota dryland farmers in 1936.

An old cedar tree stood in the front yard of the farmhouse, clinging to life but only because it was so old its roots were

buried deep beneath what had once been a little grassy yard. A pond dug by Alfred, Betty's father, and his neighbors was empty, bone dry. Once there had been tadpoles and dragonflies and frogs singing in the night, now it was just a dusty hole.

The little yard had a bent wire fence connected by a gate that would no longer close, the hinges long gone, the latch broken. The fence was useless. There were no dogs, no pets, no small children playing in that yard. It had long been given up to the hard clay dirt and the grasshoppers. Betty missed the dogs and the chirping of birds and the croaking of frogs. But most of all she missed the pond, the wet, water-filled pond.

Betty had just finished making breakfast for the family. That was her job. There were two older kids, a sister and a brother, and three younger children. The baby was due any time. Etta's babies were always big and she was never well, feeling much older than her years. The South Dakota prairie had taken its toll, as it did on all who dared to walk its paths or till the soil or try to make a living on its parched land.

Etta had been a young, vivacious girl back in Iowa before her parents homesteaded the land in South Dakota. Settlers got a section of land, 24 acres, free from the Government if they built a house and tilled the ground. Etta met Alfred at the tender age of 16; they married and set up housekeeping on the farm they claimed so many years ago. Etta's once golden hair now had streaks of grey and was pulled back in a tight bun to keep it off her neck. When long ago she danced the night away, Etta now slumbered on a bed of feathers plucked from countless chickens, ducks and geese, hand-sewn in a heavy, canvas-like material which made a mattress. Her hands were rough, her nails short and dirty, her skin looked leathery from the years of working in the fields, but her heart was always beautiful. And Etta was especially fond of 12-year-old Betty.

1936 not only brought on a depression, but there were dust storms caused by the drought, a one-two punch for the prairie people. And everything and everyone was affected by the Depression and Drought. The Peterson's poor old cow, Millie, was so skinny Betty wondered how she continued to move or give milk. She looked like a skeleton covered in hide. The chickens were almost as bad and, except for the meager scraps from the table they were given and the hoppers, they would not have survived. The crops had failed several years back and there was no use planting again. Everything, including Betty's thoughts, was all in shades of brown, drab, dull brown.

As Betty stood at the back door, she noticed what looked like a dust devil off in the distance, but it was a vehicle traveling along the old dirt road.

"Betty looks like company. Better go to the cistern and drag up some water."

"Momma, can't one of the boys get it?"

Betty would never say so, but she was afraid of the cistern. It was almost dry except for some muddy water caught when there was occasional rain. Once in a while, a rat or mouse, driven by thirst, would fall into the cistern. Many nights she would dream about that deep, dark place, waking so frightened she could not sleep and when daylight came, she would have to face her nightmare again.

"You know it's your job, Betty, and besides, the boys are busy with their own chores. Hurry now. I'm going to the house; it's getting hot already."

She watched her mother head to the kitchen to sit where she hoped to catch a breeze through the kitchen door. Her heart ached for her mom.

Betty took the bent tin bucket and went around the side of the house to face again for the second time that day the dark hole to pull up what water was available, remove anything floating in it and take it into the house. There she would boil it so that it could be used for cooking. She was a little angry as she had just finished putting up the dishes after fixing breakfast for everyone. At 12, that was her job, her life, and it seemed to Betty to be a never-ending cycle. Fade to brown.

Betty was a slight girl with dishwater blonde hair always in a bowl cut. It was as unattractive as her plain cotton dress her mother cut and sewed from a flour sack. Betty never smiled or laughed, there was no reason. She did not go to school every day but liked it when she did go.

Betty had epilepsy and if she got excited about anything, it would sometimes bring on a seizure. There was a medicine that could help but her parents could not afford it, so Betty's life consisted of cooking for the family and cleaning up afterward. Her mother depended on her more than any of the other children and Betty felt a sense of responsibility to her family.

She also knew who was coming down the road, poor, hot disenfranchised travelers. She had seen them before, people she never knew but who looked so familiar, hopeless people with their worldly possessions loaded on old vehicles heading west towards what they hoped was a better future. The less fortunate than those were the ones walking. So many tired, hungry men looking to find peace, a place away from the dirt and poverty, a place where they could provide for their families, a place with fresh air and opportunity.

She hated seeing them on that road because they reminded her of herself. That was the hard part. They were her and, it seemed it might be her future, her legacy. She pulled up the brackish water and headed to the house, careful not to spill a drop of that precious stuff.

"How is it today, honey?" Mom asked as she fanned herself with a piece of paper, the paper having come off the front of an old Sears catalog.

"What, Momma, the day or the water?"

"The water, Betty, could you tell how much is down there?"

"A little, no rats this time. I think they've all gone now." Where they went, she did not know, but she was hoping they had moved on, wishing she could go too.

Dad walked in with the three boys, Christian, the oldest at 16 the two younger boys, Albert and Daniel, 7 and 8. The other two girls, one older than Betty, Willow, 14, and one younger by one year, Gretta, were in the cellar where it was cool, having done their chores early in the day.

Betty's father was a tall, lanky man with thinning hair he parted down the middle. His clothes were ill-fitting, and he had to wear suspenders to hold up his pants. He had a quiet demeanor and never raised his voice, he learned early on it did no good to yell or get excited. It took too much energy, energy best served on the farm. He came into the kitchen to check on everyone and maybe just sit for a bit. Alfred was tired.

There was constant silt that sifted through any crack it might find and no amount of sweeping or dusting helped. The Petersons learned to live with it like so many others living on the prairie.

Betty's dad looked out the tattered screen door, taking note of a distant dust devil.

"Gonna be another scorcher today."

He stood quietly for a minute, his tall thin frame reminding Betty of all the transients that traveled this path. They all had the same look. They looked like Alfred.

"We got company coming down the road. I hate to see that 'cause we know what that means, but we need to feed 'em. Mother got the eggs, six of 'em today, so we'll feed 'em eggs and bread. Any coffee in the pot, Betty?"

"No, Papa, I'm gonna boil some water right now and get the skillet out. How many this time, Papa, can you tell?"

"Can't say yet. I don't know who's comin' down the road."

Alfred was watching the gathering dust cloud but also the sky. Something didn't look quite right today, a little hazy with an orange/brown glow and that was not a good sign. He knew what that meant. A storm was rolling in, a dust storm. There was a tiny breeze but so dry and hot it felt almost like an oven and Alfred was worried.

Chapter 2

The Travelers

The family that slowly made their way down the dirt road was known to Betty. It was Thurber, a classmate, and his family. They were piled in an old non-descript truck along with their worldly possessions. The Ford pickup truck had been painted a dark color, but rust and age had taken over its body, and it looked like it would not be able to move one more foot. The tires were worn, the running boards were about to fall off and it seemed to scream under all the weight of furniture, clothes, bedding and people.

Thurber was a nice young man about 12 years of age and Betty liked his quiet manner, old beyond his years. And she especially liked him because he was kind to her and never teased her like some of the other boys about her epilepsy.

Alfred met them at the gate as they were slowly stepping down from their rickety truck piled high with all their worldly treasures. There were six of them, three adults and three children.

"Hey folks, come on in and sit a spell. We were just about to put the coffeepot on. Sure didn't know you were movin' James. Sorry to see you leave, come on in, it's getting hot already."

The six of them, husband James, wife Phyllis, Thurber, two nondescript little ones with runny noses and dirty clothes and an elderly lady everyone called Nana came shuffling into the parlor and sat down around the heavy claw-footed oak table.

"Where you headed, James? Where can you go to find work, a place to live? What's your plan?"

James, a small, gaunt man who looked much older than his 40 or so years sat quietly, head bowed and thought for a moment. It was especially hard for this family because they were black and finding work was going to be difficult. That's the way it was for folks like James. Life was SO unfair, so unforgiving in this harsh land and it showed in his face, his demeanor.

"Don't know, Alfred. Out West, I guess. We'll look for work along the way. We got three good hands, me, Mom and Thurber. We'll get by. Ain't nothin' here for us." He slumped into the old wooden chair, took a deep breath and said, "They got our house, the land, everything Alfred. The bank is gonna auction our place off. The sheriff came out with a piece of paper, said we gotta move. We can't stay here anymore."

They had just begun their journey and were already hungry. Betty's heart broke for them, but she was too young to really express her feelings to her elders and she knew better so she went to the kitchen and Phyllis followed her to help. There were just six eggs this morning and half a loaf of bread, wrapped carefully in butcher paper. Betty had baked it the day before. That meant she would have to bake more today, but at the moment, she felt a rush of relief that they still had some flour and starter. She could be in Thurber's place.

She put kindling in the old stove, which made the kitchen hotter than blazes.

"We have a little milk left. Maybe the babies would like some."

Phyllis said in a quiet voice "they would love that. Haven't had any milk in a few days now, since the old cow died. I guess it's goin' on a week, maybe more." Each day ran into the other and there was no longer a need to keep track.

Betty took the milk, added a few precious drops of cream that had been earmarked for town and took it out to the two toddlers, then came back to get the dishes to set the table. They ate until it was gone, hardly looking up. After their meal, the little ones fell asleep on the floor and the grownups sat drinking a cup of coffee.

"James," ventured Alfred, "I don't know what's out there but it ain't good. Are you sure you should go? You know I ain't one to pry but, I mean, do you have any money? Do you have any idea where you're goin?"

"We managed to sell a few things and we got almost $7.00 for the stuff, so we got a little money for gas. All I know is we can't stay here. Our cow died a week ago Sunday, we had to eat our old chickens and you know this drought is a killer. Not much rain, nothin' here Alfred. Then there are always the black blizzards, those blasted dirt storms that are killin' all of us."

"Heading West ain't the answer, James. Maybe I could give you a couple of fertile eggs to hatch and help with the milk 'til you get back on yer feet. You won't get far with what you got." James looked down for a minute and then back at Alfred, "Remember the bank, Alfred? They want their pound of flesh."

Alfred looked out the front door towards the West and the sky was turning an ugly grey, orange color. He knew what that meant, dirt and wind like a giant furious bull pawing the parched earth, snorting and blowing and running over everything in its path. There was no stopping it and it was coming. Again.

Alfred was thoughtful for a moment with that wiser than his age look. He was not an old man, but the SD prairie he chose to homestead was trying to belch him out too. It took its' toll on all who tried to tame it. This was their destiny, the long fight.

Thurber and Betty walked out into the yard and they too stood looking to the west.

"What do you think, Thurber, is the weather gonna be bad?"

Betty could feel it in her slight, thin little body. The air hung heavy and it was far too quiet; even the very slight breeze stopped to catch sight of what was now looming in the distance. Willow and Gretta came up from the root cellar where Gretta had been cutting up a Montgomery Wards' catalog to make paper dolls. Willow was looking through the new catalog making her wish list. Betty did not play or make wishes, she had her chores and Mother needed help all the time now. The baby was due anytime and it was going to be a big one. All of Ettas' babies were big, but this one was different. Mother felt ill the whole time she was pregnant and could hardly manage even the simplest things. It was exhausting for her to walk across the yard. Even when Betty wasn't in the same room, she could hear her mother groaning under the strain of carrying another baby in a time when babies were not so much joy as a burden.

"Hi Thurber, what're you doin' here?" asked Gretta, a smaller version of Betty. She had the same blond hair cut straight around just below the ears, the same small frame, the same blue eyes. She was a Peterson.

Betty felt a little angry that both the girls had not even known about the company until all the hard work was done but then her resentment flew away like the old crow on its way to greener parts. She was always protective of her sisters in a motherly way.

"Hi Gretta, we're movin' today. Ain't stayin here not one more day."

"Why Thurber, I thought you liked it here."

"Naw, it's no good here. We're goin' West to California maybe or Washington or Oregon. There are jobs and good food and money to be had out West."

He did not sound very convincing because deep down inside, he knew the truth and he could have cried, except it wasn't "manly."

From inside the house came the sound of some commotion. Thurber, Betty, Gretta and Willow ran in to see what was going on. Sitting on a chair was Mother and she was in labor.

Etta whispered more to herself than anyone, " Oh Lord, not yet. I ain't ready for this baby."

The sky took on an ugly, ominous color, the color of dried earth on the move. They were getting a storm and another mouth to feed. But come hades or high water, both were on the way.

Chapter 3

Before the Storm

"Where's the rest of the kids?" Etta asked as Betty and Thurber's mom, Phyllis helped her to the bedroom. Alfred ran to the back door and yelled for the boys, Christian, Albert and Daniel. Christian was rounding up the hens and the two younger boys were out at the barn throwing rocks at the scrawny birds who hoped to grab a bite from some of the equally scrawny chickens.

"Come in, boys, it's gonna get bad out there. Storm's a-comin'".

The wind was starting to pick up and the air was heavy. It had a metallic smell, the smell of burnt earth, dirt heated up by the sun, each little particle dancing in a roiling, ugly journey to wherever the wind chose to drop it. That was their lot in life.

The boys ran in and immediately were handed some rags. They had to be put up against windows and doors, stuffed in as many cracks as possible, otherwise the dust would win again. Everyone got busy and in the back bedroom you could hear Etta starting the ritual of birth.

It was SO hot in that house with no air coming in. Betty felt she might faint from lack of oxygen but there was no alternative. They had to keep out the weather.

"Dad, would it be better to go to the cellar? It's cooler down there. Mother is going to get way too hot up here. Can we move her?"

Alfred thought for a moment and then went to the bedroom to talk to the women. When he came back, he called everyone together.

"It's a bit too late to move mom, but I want the rest of you, except me, Betty and Phyllis to head to the cellar. There are candles down there and it's cooler. You will be fine 'til the storm passes and then I will come get you. James will be there to watch out for you so go, NOW."

With that, the boys pulled the rags from around the back door again and everyone, the grandmother, the small children, Thurber, Gretta, Willow, Christian, Albert, Daniel, and James ran out the back towards the cellar door. The wind had picked up and it was getting hard to see. The dirt hit them in the face and arms, which stung like needles. They all knew it was going to be a big storm.

When everyone had gotten to the cellar safely and the rickety wooden door was shut behind them, Alfred turned his attention to the back door of the kitchen again. He packed rags around it as best he could and checked the rest of the house. It didn't much matter though, dirt was filtering in from everywhere and the wind was beginning to howl outside.

Alfred looked at Betty and his heart broke. She was so frail, so tiny and yet had so much responsibility on her 12year-old shoulders. The older children were a big help but not like Betty. She had a maturity far beyond her years and she knew what it was like to be caught in a dust storm. Betty had been out in the pasture trying to get the old cow in the barn when one hit. The old cow saved her life. Betty grabbed the cow's tail and let her lead the way. The cow, Millie, had come back to the barn only by instinct, but it proved miraculous for Betty, who could not even see her hand in front of her face. Her family was waiting anxiously for the storm to be over so they could hunt for her. They found her in the barn curled up in a corner, alive but wheezing from breathing in that fine silicate dust. It would be that way for her from then on and Betty became the house child, the one everyone depended on to help Mother, to keep the house in order, to be there for them and she was, always. Between her weakened lungs and her epilepsy, she had little choice but to lead a rather dull existence but one she took on with her sense of responsibility.

Betty and Alfred moved to the back bedroom, where Etta was in labor. Phyllis was sitting by her side, holding her hand. When they came into the room, Phyllis looked up at the two with a serious worried look that told them something was not quite right.

"How's it going, Mamma" although Alfred already knew it was not going well.

Phyllis looked at him again and said, "Alfred, we need the Dr. The baby is not wanting to be born and Etta is almost ready to deliver."

"We can't leave yet, Phyllis. The storm is raging right now and I know the old truck wouldn't make it. The dust would just choke the engine. How much longer do you think?"

"Past time."

Just then, Etta, who was pale and sweaty, let out a pure instinctual sound, something they had not heard from her before, a low, groan, more animal than human.

"I need more water, at least Alfred. Can you get me more water?"

Betty, who had been standing near the door, spoke up for the first time,

"I can go get it, Daddy, you know I know my way around out there like the back of my hand. I can do it."

"You'll get lost out there, Betty. I can't let you go."

They both looked over at Etta, struggling now to even breathe; she was so weak. The wind howled outside like a pack of mad dogs and when Alfred turned back to Betty, she was gone. He knew that she was determined to do it for her mother, for her baby brother or sister, but he hadn't wanted her to go. Now he had two to worry about, no three, the new baby too.

Betty grabbed an old shirt from a hook hanging by the backdoor and removed the rags stuffed around the door frame. She took an old tea towel and wrapped it around her mouth and nose. She could hear the wind trying to tear the house down, so angry, howling at its own inability to destroy and rip the land, knowing its time was brief but vicious in its attempt to tear everything apart in its path before it died.

She took the old bucket in her hand and started to feel her way to the cistern. She knew this by heart because it had been a game for her. Feel the back door and walk straight forward 20 steps, 20 Betty steps. Keep your eyes closed! Then turn to the left and walk another 30 steps. Betty steps. On the right hand is the lid to the cistern, an old wooden one ready to fall apart both from the weather and the hoppers eating it.

"Tie the rope to the handle of the bucket, lower it and get what water is available, she thought." The wind tore at her legs and pulled at her dress. So angry it was, it tried to pull her dress off her shoulders. She could feel the dirt in her hair; it was getting under her face cover and into her mouth, her eyes, everywhere. She finally managed to pull up whatever water she could, not much, and it would have to be boiled. Mom was running out of time and Betty was very afraid for her.

The wind was at her back going into the house and it almost threw her into the kitchen, it was that angry. Alfred was waiting for her and took the bucket, having already started a fire in the old stove. He was using cow pies for cooking with because of the shortage of wood. He strained the water and put it on to boil while Betty shook the dirt from her hair, her clothes, her mouth, her eyes. There was nowhere that had been spared.

"Betty, I need you to go sit with Mother. I'll be right in."

Alfred thought he heard someone at the back door. "Couldn't be. The kids are in the cellar. Nobody in their right mind is out in this stuff" he thought. "Must be the wind."

Again there was a banging at the door, so Alfred undid the rags again and peered out to see what or who it was. There in the haze stood Lloyd.

Chapter 4

Lloyd

"Lloyd, get yer butt out that door and get them hogs put up. The weather's comin' in. Do it RIGHT NOW!"

Lloyd was a small, skinny boy of 13 with blond hair and blue eyes. His eyes were like small pools of water, pale and glassy with never a hint of what lay beneath. He lived with his father, Lucas, on a small, rundown farm and life for Lloyd was hard. His mother had left the year before and took his two sisters with her. She left Lloyd on that desolate patch of earth, not looking back and she had been Lloyd's world, his protection from his father, Lucas. She escaped; he did not.

Now there was no buffer, no insulator from a hateful, mean-spirited man who had no time for his son or anyone else. Lloyd was a loner and because of Lucas, he was bullied by some of the other kids and picked on by some of the older men, men who had had dealings with Lloyd's father. Most in the area knew Lucas and he was not well-liked. That meant that Lloyd was just a by-product of Lucas standing in the community.

"And, oh yeah, your horse is looking puny. We can't feed that old nag anymore. You need to shoot him. If you don't do it, I will."

Today was going to be a bad one. Dad was in a vile mood and so was the weather. Best to keep out of everyone's way. As Lloyd headed out of the house toward the rundown old barn, he saw his horse, Scout, running around wildly, throwing his head. Scout was not a pretty horse. He was white with big blue splotches under his coat, his head was way too big for his body and he was skinny, but that's what drew Lloyd to Scout. They were two of a kind, misfits, skinny, dirty, unloved by others, but Lloyd loved his horse, his best and only friend.

"What's the matter, old man? I'm gonna be back just as soon as those hogs are put in the barn. Don't worry; I won't leave you and I sure as heck won't shoot you. We'll run away first, buddy."

Lloyd looked at the sky and it reeked of dirt and promises of furious things to come. The earth was angry and it knew how to let people know. If only Lloyd could let people know how angry he was, he would be as strong and destructive as the wind. Someday.

He got the two stubborn old hogs inside and turned to Scout.

"Come on, old man, let's get in the barn. I'll stay with ya', come on."

And with that, he grabbed Scout's halter and tried to steer him into the barn. Scout would have none of it and broke away from Lloyd. The old wooden gate had blown open and Scout, seeing his chance at freedom, bolted and he was off running wildly terrified of what was coming upon them but excited by his newfound freedom. The prairie beckoned.

Lloyd stood silent for a moment wanting to cry, but he didn't. Instead, he took out after his horse barefoot across the dry, barren, ugly landscape.

Scout ran a half-mile full bore until he came to Betty's homestead. There he decided to stop and look for something to eat. He was always hungry, just like everything else in this barren, nondescript land.

"You cantankerous old piss-poor excuse for a horse."

Lloyd, out of breath from running a half-mile in the looming storm, shouted at Scout, all the while petting him and hugging him, so great was his fear that he'd lost his best friend.

The wind blew hard and everything was turning grey-brown as the earth gave up its lifeblood. Everything was getting covered with fine, dry dust and it was getting hard to breathe, so Lloyd took Scout into the Peterson's barn to find some protection there.

He carefully tied Scout to a post in a corner that gave him a little protection from what was to come, and Lloyd would have stayed with him except he noticed a form moving in the yard. Worried about who might be out in the coming weather, Lloyd left Scout and headed towards the disappearing figure. As he got closer, he tried yelling to the small girl struggling with a bucket, trying to stay on her feet as the storm got worse. He knew it was Betty as she slipped in the back door. He stood for a minute, trying to decide whether to turn around and try to find the barn again or go on up to the house. He needed to make up his mind; the wind, the dirt, his very existence was hanging in the balance. He moved as best he could to the back door and knocked. No answer. He banged on the door, afraid now nobody would hear him. People have died in these storms and he knew that was a serious possibility.

Mr. Peterson came to the door and let Lloyd in.

"Lloyd! Where'd you come from, boy? You shouldn't be out in this stuff, how'd you get here?"

Lloyd looked down, ashamed of his apparent misstep, and noticed his feet were bleeding. So did Alfred.

"My horse took off Mr. Peterson and I ran after him. I hope you don't mind, but I tied him up in your barn. I'll leave as soon as the weather clears, I promise."

"It's OK, Lloyd, you ran all the way from your place? Look at you covered in dirt. Come in and we'll get you a drink of water. Come on now."

"Thank you, sir, I don't need no water. I'm fine."

He was very thirsty but didn't want to bother anyone; he just wanted to stay for a little while and then he would have to figure out where he was going. It wasn't back to the homestead. His Dad would for sure make him shoot Scout.

From the other room came a low-pitched cry and the sound startled Lloyd.

"We're havin' a baby, Lloyd. That's the misses. You'll have to excuse me, it's getting real close."

And with that, he was gone. Lloyd found a chair and sat quietly, listening to the commotion coming from the other room as the world groaned outside. Both were in serious trouble.

Alfred slipped into the bedroom and moved over to his wife's side. She was struggling and he could tell it was not going well, not for her or the baby. Betty was holding her hand and when Etta had a contraction, she would squeeze Betty's hand so hard it made her wince, but she would not remove her hand from her mother's nor let her mom know it hurt. Phyllis was at the foot of the bed and, in the gloom, couldn't really tell what was happening.

"Alfred, bring that lamp over here, hurry."

Alfred lit the kerosene lamp and held it for Phyllis.

"Lord have mercy! I just don't know what to do for Etta. She needs to push but she's not having this baby."

Phyllis was not a midwife and even though she had helped birth animals on the farm, she had never helped birth a child before.

Lloyd came to the door when he heard the commotion. He stood there knowing this was the end of the world and they were all in hell. The wind was howling outside and it must be 110 degrees in the closed-up old house. The earth was trying to bury them, alive or dead, it didn't matter. "What had they done to deserve this?" he wondered to himself.

Betty came out of the bedroom looking pale and shaken.

"What's wrong, Betty? Is everything OK?"

"Oh hey Lloyd, no, somethin's wrong, bad wrong. Mom can't have this baby and we need Dr. Hoyt here right now. Poor Phyllis is crazy scared and Papa is frantic. We can't use the truck, we wouldn't get out of the yard with this dirt blowin' so hard."

Lloyd thought for a minute, "Betty, I could go to town and get the Doc. I can go on Scout. He knows the way and the wind would be at our back. We could do it."

"No, Lloyd, you can't get out in this stuff, it's too dangerous, and besides, there's no way to tell if the doc could even get back out here. No! you can't go."

But Lloyd was already making plans.

"I could put those blinders hanging in the barn on Scout to help with the dirt and I could borrow a towel to wrap around my head. I can do it, Betty. Your Mamma needs help."

Betty looked at Lloyd and knew that really was the only answer.

"OK, Lloyd, but I'm goin' too."

"You can't go, Betty; your mom needs you right now."

"She's got everyone here to help. We will both go." Her mind was made up too.

"You need to tell your Dad Betty."

"No, I'm not telling anyone. Let's go then before it gets any worse."

Betty grabbed some old dishtowels off the rack, took the boiled water off the stove, closed the damper on the stove so the fire would go out and off they went into hell.

Holding hands, they made it to the barn where Scout was tied. The wind howled like a banshee and they had to yell at each other to be heard.

"Lloyd, how do you know Scout will head to town. He might go the other way."

"Betty he'll take us to town, that's where he gets a carrot or a few oats or something. He'll get us there."

With that, they found the blinders and a worn leather feed bag. Lloyd put both on Scout to help keep out the dirt. He didn't have a saddle but they found an old blanket, threw it over Scout's back and climbed up. They tied the dishtowels around their necks and pulled them up over their noses. Betty had some old goggles she gave to Lloyd, so she just had to keep her eyes closed against the storm.

Chapter 5

Into the Storm

Scout went slowly, reluctantly into that windy nightmare. He was skittish and the dirt pelted all three of them like stinging nettles, but Etta and that baby's life depended on them.

Scout put his head down and turned away from the wind and headed toward town. The kids could barely keep the towels from being blown off and they did little good anyway. It was a mile and a half down dirt roads to Murdo and Dr. Hoyt's office. Betty put her arms around Lloyd's waist, putting her head behind his back, trying to hide from the dirt. He wore the goggles.

The town was a small collection of buildings set in the middle of the prairie. There was a grocery store run by the grocer, Mr. Robertson. The store had a unique smell like ripe vegetables, oil that was spread on the worn, wooden floors to keep the dust down and bath and laundry soaps which consisted of Life Bouy and Fels Naptha. Next to the grocer on the corner was a restaurant, Mac's Cafe. That's where the town's people met every Saturday night after the movie at the local theatre.

It was the theatre that was the most exciting.

The last movie Betty saw was King Kong starring Fay Wray and Betty's secret heart throb: Robert Armstrong. It was so frightening!

Everyone was screaming right along with Fay Wray all the way through the movie but Betty cried at the end when King Kong got killed. It was very traumatic and Betty thought she might be sick and as it turned out, she had a seizure later that night. It was SO worth it, though.

Across the street stood the Post Office which was always filled with cigar smoke, Old Spice aftershave and newspaper ink, making it totally male territory. The older men around town met there to discuss the latest news and, even though it was never mentioned, to gossip.

Another one of Betty's favorite places was the Five and Dime. She loved to look at all the wonderful things that lay nestled in neat little bins, tiny doll babies she could make clothes for and small trucks and cars. She could not afford any of those things, they cost as much as five to ten cents each and silver money was hard to come by. Sometimes Betty dreamed of finding money laying in the gutter, clear water running over a glittering pile of silver. In her dream, she would grab what she could before it fell down the drain, but then she woke and realized it was only a dream, and she always woke up.

Next to the Five and Dime was the best place of all, the drug store. When she opened the big glass door with the words "Wheat's Drug Store" written on it, a bell tinkled, alerting Mr. Wheat, the druggist, that there were customers. The soda fountain, a massive hand-carved wooden bar where cherry cokes and chocolate malts were served, was in the back of the store where one of the local boys was busy behind the counter, ready to make whatever your heart desired, whatever you could afford. The boy on duty was called the "soda jerk" and Betty thought that was a bit insulting, but the young men wore that title with pride. Betty had to walk through the store to get to the soda fountain. What a wonderful adventure to wander the aisles with the magazines and coloring books along with cutout paper dolls. Then there were the bottles full of things that were as mysterious as their names. "Midnight in Paris".

Down Main Street, an unpaved, rutted road stood the Gamble's store that had a new rubber tire smell and anything a farmer or handyman might need. That place had been there since the beginning of time and would probably exist long after all the others were gone. Next to the Gamble's store was a little white house with an old tree that grew way too close to the building in the front yard. There was a small white picket fence which was whitewashed yearly. The house was their target; that's where Dr. Hoyt lived and had his practice. That's where they were headed.

"Oh, POOP" yelled Betty over the wind and into Lloyd's back.

"What did you say, Betty?" yelled Lloyd, who only heard a muffled sound through the towel.

"I said POOP, you know, crap!"

"You can't swear like that, Betty. Girls don't say that stuff."

"Well, I can and I do! POOP, POOP, POOP and besides, you cuss."

"No I don't, Betty, least ways not around women."

"I've heard you say crap. That's swearin', Lloyd."

"Is NOT,Betty, at least not for me" he yelled back.

"Is so Lloyd."

"Is NOT Betty."

"Is TOO."

"NOT."

"TOO"

And so it went, both yelling at each other until suddenly they realized the wind had quieted a bit. And in the distance an outline of some buildings, TOWN!!!!

Scout saw it too and picked up his speed. He went from 0 to 2 in a short time. He was also trying to divest himself of his feedbag because it was empty. He was shaking his head from side to side and up and down. They came to Main Street only to find it deserted. Nobody in their right mind was out today. Even the Post Office was closed. Doc. Hoyt HAD to be home. They made their way down the dirt-filled street until they saw the little white house with the tree growing too close to it. The tree was straggly and bare of leaves and might even have been dead, but there it was a sure sign they had found their way. Scout proved to be a true thoroughbred, not the old nag Lloyd's Dad said he was.

Both jumped off the horse and ran for the little white picket fence surrounding the yard. On reaching the front door, both of them banged on it at the same time, desperate now to see the Dr.

"Well, what in the world? Kids, what are you doing out in this stuff?"

"Doc, Doc, you gotta come quick, Betty's mom is having that baby right now and she's havin' a hard time. Please, hurry." Lloyd's breath came in spurts; there was so little oxygen in the air.

"Oh Lord, let me get my bag. I'll crank up the car and you can tie your horse behind. What a time to have a baby, Etta," he mumbled while he ran for his things.

Outside, the storm had quieted a bit. The wind was still blowing dirt around, but it was not the blizzard it had been, a good sign that things were going to get better, at least a short break for them.

Dr. Hoyt was trying to get his car out of a lean-to next to the house but it wouldn't budge, wouldn't turn over, wouldn't start. After about ten agonizing minutes, he gave up.

"Can't get the dad-blasted thing to start, kids. I'm at a loss here."

"We could all go back on Scout Doc. He'll get us there." There was such a sincere look on Lloyd's face and such determination in his eyes, that Dr. Hoyt agreed.

"You know it's been YEARS since I straddled a horse, kids. You'll have to lead the way."

"Doc, you wouldn't happen to have a piece of bread or something for Scout, would you? He'd do lots better if he had something to chew on."

"Well, Lloyd, I just do happen to have something he'll really like, an apple. Just got it from the store yesterday, nice and fresh too."

Dr. Hoyt ran into the house and returned with a shiny, bright red apple. Such a treasure was hard to come by and very expensive! They put it in the feedbag and that made Scout happy. They all three got on that old horse's back and with the Doctor's bag in hand, they headed back to the farm. The kids felt it would be alright then. There was hope in the air.

Chapter 6

Back to the Farm

The trip home was quicker since the wind had died down a bit. Betty was grateful it was a quick storm as some raged on for days, but there was still an unsettled urgency in the air.

Scout would only go so fast no matter how much Lloyd yelled, pulled, kicked or cajoled. As they got to the old farmhouse, Betty could see the group coming up from the cellar led by James, Thurber's dad. Phyllis must still be in the house helping Betty's mom with the birthing.

Betty was first to jump off Scout, followed by the Doctor and then Lloyd. She went running in ahead of everyone but was stopped at the bedroom door by Phyllis. There was total silence, but Phyllis' face spoke volumes. She was ashen and her hands trembled. She could not look at Betty directly but kept glancing around as if she were a caged animal wanting to escape.

"Ms. Phyllis, how is mother? What about the baby? Is it born yet?"

The Dr. arrived and Phyllis turned from Betty and opened the door for him. Betty tried to slip in after him, but she was stopped.

"Ms. Phyllis, what's happening? Please, tell me." There was no answer but that silence brought sheer terror to Betty.

The Doctor came to the door and motioned for Betty to enter the bedroom. Her Mom wanted to see her. Betty went to the bed where her mother was lying holding a newborn baby. The baby was quiet, too quiet and still, so very still.

"Mamma?" Betty whispered.

"Betty, honey, the baby didn't make it. He's gone, sweetheart."

Betty stood there for a moment, trying to make sense of it all and could not.

"You mean I'm too late, Mamma? "

"No, honey, you were not too late. The baby was just too early. It's a little brother Betty."

She stood silently for a moment, trying to make sense of it all even though there is no sense in death.

"Can I hold him, Mamma?"

"If you want to, Betty." And with that, she held out this tiny bundle wrapped in a small quilt Etta had made months before from old clothes and pieces of fabric she had saved.

Betty took the precious bundle and hugged him tightly. He looked so peaceful; his little eyes shut as if he was sleeping, his wispy blond hair lying against his perfectly shaped little head. He had his hand up against his face. He seemed like he was about to open his eyes any second to this old world, this vicious, uncaring world.

"He needs a name, Mamma, what's his name?" She looked at his little face, so peaceful, so perfect.

"It was supposed to be Frederick, Frederick Emil. That's what we will call him."

The silence was deafening. There was no crying, venting, raging, no swearing or fist-shaking at the Powers-that-Be, only the silence. And nobody was blaming God. How could someone blame Him for something that was so human? Not His fault, not anybody's fault, just a fact of life out here and it was just accepted.

"Jesus loves me this I know for the Bible tells me so, little ones to him belong, they are weak but he is strong, yes Jesus loves me, yes Jesus loves me, yes Jesus loves me, the Bible tells me so."

Betty sang an age-old song to her baby brother in her small, little girl voice, told him how sorry she was and that they had tried really hard to make it back in time. And she said she loved him.

"We will see him again, honey" and with that, the Doctor gently lifted the little boy from Betty's arms making ready to take him to town and prepare for burial.

Town? Dr. Hoyt realized he had no way to get back to town except on Scout. How was he going to manage that?

"Oh my, I have no way to get back to town, not with this baby anyway."

He stepped out of the bedroom to find everyone that had been in the cellar waiting quietly in the living room. There was James' family, Phyllis, who was sitting, staring out a dirty unwashed window, the curtains gently moving to the beat of the wind outside. Thurber and James, father and husband, sat on the chairs around the table. The grandmother and Betty's siblings were on an overstuffed couch. Betty came out and sat down on the floor next to Lloyd. Nobody said a word. The world had stopped turning.

"James, could I impose upon you to drive me to town?"

"Oh sure, Dr. Hoyt, I'd be more than happy to help you out."

James thought about how limited his resources were. They had been on their way hopefully to a new life since their farm was about to be repossessed, but this was something that he had to do and Phyllis knew it. The Foley family would figure something out later; this was important, more important than the harrowing trip they were starting.

"I will be back for you in a little bit, kids," James told them and with that, the two men prepared to leave, Doctor Hoyt holding that precious bundle.

The rickety Model A truck was loaded with all the Foley family's worldly possessions and there was hardly any space to sit. Doctor Hoyt wondered at this with all the folks that had been riding in the vehicle but he said nothing. He held Frederick, now totally covered by the quilt on his lap. The truck started after a few tries and took off down the dirt-blown rutted trail. There was silence again because it was an unwritten rule that men did not cry nor ever discuss their true feelings with each other. The same unwritten word told them to be staunch, strong and silent. That was the way it was. The Petersons would bury their little one with nary a word about it and go on trying to scratch a living from a dead earth that just wanted to spit, to vomit it all out. This same dead earth would welcome another one in a day or so, turning a once-living thing into exactly what it was, dust. "From dust, you were made and to dust, you will return" and there was nothing anyone could do about it. The wind had died down and all was quiet, blanketed in a fine, light powder.

Chapter 7

The Real Deal

Lloyd had taken Scout back out to the barn, where he gently brushed him off, took off the blinders and feedbag that had protected him from the storm and tried to find something for him to eat. There was a little hay but it had a dry rot in it that was not good for the animals. Lloyd proceeded to pick through it and find what he could that was not too dusty or too moldy to feed Scout. They were both hungry, the skinny little boy and the equally skinny horse that was his best friend.

"Lloyd, what are you doing, son?" Betty's dad asked. He startled Lloyd, walking in quietly. But then Alfred was a quiet man.

"Uh, oh hi Mr. Peterson, I'm feeding Scout a little bit of your hay. I hope you don't mind, he's had a rough day."

"You go on ahead and feed him, Lloyd, you're welcome to anything we have here and I brought you both a drink of water from the cistern. It's been boiled, so it's good."

Lloyd started to refuse but he was so thirsty and he knew Scout was too so he accepted the glass bottle filled with water, gave most of it to Scout in a bucket and drank a little himself.

"What's your plan, Lloyd? You got one? Betty tells me you won't go home, why not?"

Lloyd looked down in deep thought for a minute and then looked up at the tall man in front of him.

"Mr. Peterson, if I go home I'm gonna have to shoot Scout. Dad says we can't keep him anymore, he eats too much and he doesn't help out around the farm so I'm not going back, never." There was a look of determination on the small boy's face.

"Where will you go, boy?"

"I thought I might go see my mom and sisters, they live in Mitchell, you know. Moved and left us."

"I heard Lloyd and I'm sorry about that, but your mom had to have a reason for leaving, didn't she?"

"Yeah, I guess so. You know she has a suiter? He's a rich man and he buys her and the girls things. I'm gonna get a job and help them out too. I'm gonna buy my mom things like pretty dresses and perfume and a box of candy."

"Right now, your job is to help your Pop."

Then there was a moment of silence where both the man and the boy just kind of looked at each other without really seeing the other one.

Alfred broke the silence then.

"I talked to Mrs. Peterson a while ago and we decided we need a horse around here. Not a real workhorse but one that the kids could ride and one that knows his way to town. Do you know of a horse like that, Lloyd? We'd be willing to pay, say $2.00 for a horse like that and he could stay here with us. Of course, we'd need a boy to help take care of him." Alfred put his hand to his chin and looked perplexed.

"I DO know a horse just like that, Mr. Peterson, Scout!" For the first time, there was a hint of hope in Lloyd's eyes. "And I know a boy who would take care of him for free, ME!"

"Yep, and you could take the money to your Dad for feed for the hogs."

"But do you have that kind of money, Mr. Peterson? That's a lot."

"Mrs. Peterson has some egg money saved up, so we're good. We have a burial here in the next few days but we'll work that out with the Doc. What do you say, Lloyd? You want to sell Scout?"

"Yes sir, yes I would. He'd be safe here with you, and I would come over every day to help take care of him, and then when I get enough money, I could buy him back."

"That you could, Lloyd."

They shook hands, the deal sealed. It was the real deal and Alfred handed Lloyd $2.00 in change and Scout was now part of the Peterson clan.

"You need to head home son, your Pa is probably wondering where you're at."

"He's gonna be mad but when he sees the money, it'll be OK. See you tomorrow, Mr. Peterson, early."

And without another word, Lloyd set off across the prairie for home, secure in the knowledge that his best friend, his only friend, was safe. He'd saved Scout and he was happy. It was almost dark and Lloyd had a half-mile to walk.

Alfred went back in the house. Everyone was sitting in the living room, the kids wrapped around the old oak table, the lantern had been lit. Nobody was really saying too much, but Alfred knew it was time to feed everyone. Normally Etta would go kill an old rooster and then Betty would fry it up in a big cast-iron skillet but Etta was in her bed and Betty had to go lay down herself. Betty felt like she might have one of her seizures after all the excitement and pain of the day. It was also time for chores. Everyone and everything had a schedule and today was no exception.

"Kids, just to let you know, Momma and I are keeping Scout for a bit. You treat the old guy as you would any of our animals and Lloyd will come over to help take care of him. He's in the barn and he's part of this here farm now. Understand?"

They all nodded and stood to go about their business, each one knowing what his job was. Phyllis, who had been reflecting out the one and only window in the sitting room, got up and headed for the barnyard. Without a word, she knew it was up to her to get dinner for almost a dozen people, including small children. Finding enough food was going to be a chore in itself.

．　．　．

Lloyd arrived home after dark. Luther was sitting by an old oil lamp that dimly lit the room.

"Where the hell you been? Been waiting all afternoon, Lloyd. I had to feed the hogs myself. You better have a good excuse."

"I do papa, Scout ran out of the pen this morning and I chased him all the way to Peterson's place. Then we got caught in the storm, so had to wait 'til it was clear. Look! Petersons' bought Scout and gave me a whole $1.50 for him. Here's the money so you can buy feed for the hogs." With that, he counted out exactly $1.50 and handed it to Lucas.

"Saves a bullet now, doesn't it" was all he said. He took the money and walked off.

Lloyd was feeling bad about lying to his Dad and secretly keeping some of the money he got from Mr. Peterson, but he had an agenda and he needed it worse than those old hogs right now. He was going to see his mom and bring her a box of chocolates. As sad as the day was, Lloyd was happy to think he might make his momma happy, if even for a short while. He had plans to make. He was going to see his family and bring them presents!!!

Chapter 8

Spread the Word

Word quickly spread through the small, tight-knit community that the Petersons had lost their baby. Times were hard, so there was a different kind of compassion, an unspoken understanding that each neighbor would do his best to help the family in need. The Foley's stayed the night at the farm so Phyllis could help Etta.

The following morning the Petersons could see the dust being kicked up by horses, wagons and model T and model A vehicles, all coming to pay respects and grieve with the family. Each visiting family brought something to eat, whatever they had and that helped more than anything. The night before, Phyllis had managed to catch an old rooster, wring his neck, clean the innards, pluck the feathers and fry it up for the brood. There should have been at least two chickens to feed everyone, but all got something. There was even a jar of pickles in the shelter and a jar of green beans that had been put away for almost a year but were still good. The boys milked the old cow, and they had fresh milk for the Foley babies. AND to top it off, she was able to whip up the cream that had been separated from the milk and found a jar of apples Etta had set aside so there was dessert.

Etta was still on her bed and Betty had gone in to be with her when the company started arriving. Both were silent, bound by a common pain that they knew would never leave them. Betty held her Mom's hand but did not look at her. Betty could not bear the suffering she saw in her momma's eyes, a reflection of Betty's own sorrow. They could hear the commotion outside the bedroom and realized that the poor little house was probably packed now with the busy folks that had come to pay respects to the Peterson family. Etta and Betty could smell all the food they brought and could hear the chatter as the women got things ready. It was an unwritten law. The friends and neighbors, all with the same objective, cared for this family as the Petersons had cared for them in the past.

James had not made it back the night before but Phyllis was not worried. He had driven Doctor Hoyt back to town and by the time they got there, it was probably too dark to risk coming back to the farm. She knew he would be welcome in town and so it was that he stayed the night at the Doctor's house.

"Betty, help me up, honey. Bring me a robe if you can find one."

"Momma, you need to rest, you know that."

But Betty knew her mother, knew her determination, her drive. This was the woman that had birthed seven children, ran the household, helped with the chores, milked the cows, tended a garden when there was a garden and took hold of everything that needed her attention so she dutifully got her mother a robe hanging on a hook behind the door and helped her sit up and get ready to greet her guests. Etta would never have thought to do otherwise.

It was so hot and with so many bodies in the house, it became almost impossible to stay inside. The children all ran outside to play the games they knew. Several boys, including Thurber, Albert and Christian, decided to explore the dam area. It was dry, but there were treasures there. Christian found a real fossil once, a shell he kept in his private lockbox. The little girls found some shade under that scruffy old evergreen and started playing Cats Cradle, a game that one girl would start by using string wrapped around her fingers. She would make something with the string and pass it off to the next girl. Whoever made the Cats' Cradle won.

A few of the children went down to the shelter where Gretta and Willow had an old Montgomery Wards catalog with which they would cut out paper dolls. They had their models, their clothes and even some furniture, all from a dream book that ultimately went to the outhouse.

The men from the community, almost a dozen, stepped outside for a smoke and the most recent talk. James had returned, bringing the Methodist Minister, brother Jones with him. They all moved up to the barn. There was business to discuss.

Alfred stood for a moment, contemplating what he was about to say. There was so much to talk about and so little the quiet man wanted to say.

"You all know how much we, the missus and I, appreciate your coming out like this, just spur of the moment." That would be as much as he could say about the death of baby Frederick.

"We all know that the Foleys have been havin' a hard time of it and you know, can I say it, James? James nodded. James and the family are losing the homestead. You all know his family's been here since our folks came here. We came in covered wagons, we walked and we pushed and pulled our wagons and we built this place, all of us with our sweat and tears and hard work. We got the land if we homesteaded it and lived on it and built on it. We did that, including James and his folks. It ain't right he's being kicked off his land by people who don't even care about it."

Alfred cleared his throat and looked down at his dusty, worn boots.

"I got an idea about this and I need your help. You know the bank's soon gonna auction his farm off to the highest bidder. It's an absolute auction which means their place goes to the highest bidder no matter what the offer, no minimum. What if we got all our money together and let James be the only one to bid on his land? What if there wasn't anybody else to bid against him? He could get his land back."

Alfred looked at the faces of each of the men one by one to get a reaction. There was silence and then one of the men spoke. It was Martin Jones, the Methodist minister.

"You know they send a man out from the bank to those auctions to bid against us and raise the price. How can we get around that?"

"Good question, Martin and I think I have an answer, but I can't talk about it right now. I have a plan that I'm pretty sure will work. What do you say, can we take up a collection? If we do this, James and his family can go back to their homestead and wait 'til the auction."

James was overcome with emotion watching the men in his community dipping into their pockets pulling out everything they had. That included the Methodist minister, the local druggist and the postmaster. Brother Jones mentioned that this was probably sinful and not to say too much more to him and hopefully, Jesus would understand and forgive them all.

Lloyd came over early to check on Scout and tell him he'd be gone for a while. He was going to hop the train that ran through town to go see his mom and he had the money to buy her a nice present, but when the men gathered out by the barn, his curiosity got the best of him, so he walked over to listen feeling pretty good about being there with the grown men. When Mr. Peterson asked for donations and the men started to put money into Alfred's hat, Lloyd knew what he had to do.

He stepped up to Alfred and took out the .50 cents he'd hidden from his father, the money to buy his mom a present, to buy her admiration and maybe her love. He put it in the hat along with the rest and stepped away. His dreams of seeing her again were dashed, but Lloyd knew if you were a man and you lived on the South Dakota prairie, you did what you had to do. It was survival for all of them.

The total of all the men had was $37.50, not much but like Alfred said, this was going to be an absolute auction, come heck or highwater, the farm was going to the highest bidder. And Alfred had a plan.

Chapter 9

A Plan of Sorts

Betty came out to the barn to see what the commotion was all about. She found Lloyd in the barn with Scout. Lloyd was sitting in a corner behind the horse, crying silently with his head bent and his knees up to his chest.

"You trying to disappear, Lloyd?" asked Betty.

He did not answer, nor did he look up. Betty sat down next to him and he moved away a bit. He wanted to be alone, he wanted to curl up in his sadness to have it surround him like a cocoon to protect him from the world that, at the moment, seemed so cruel.

"Go away, Betty, I'm just tired. I have been up a long time."

"I know better, Lloyd, what's up?"

"I'm just missing my mom and sisters, that's all. I was gonna go see them but changed my mind."

"Why did you change your mind? If you want to go see them, go."

"I will someday. Just not right now."

His heart was breaking but he knew he did the right thing by giving his money to help the Foley family. He only wished his mom would have taken him with her when she left.

He remembered the day she packed her things and threw what little she had in the car. His dad sat in the kitchen unmoving, staring out at nothing. Lloyd came in to beg his father to stop her but Lucas ignored him. His mother put his two sisters in the car and started to drive away. Lloyd came running out after her.

"Don't leave me, Mom, please, let me go too."

She never looked back, never said a word, just drove away.

He wanted so badly to be away from this dismal, distressing place, to see some flowers, to smell rain again, to ride Scout over fields of wild grass and down hilly country roads and stop to fish in a dam full of water. But most of all, he wanted his family. None of it was possible.

Betty sat silently by his side for a few minutes and then quietly put her arm around his shoulders. He started to sob. He hated himself for doing that in front of her but he couldn't help it. Scout came over and put his big ugly nose on Lloyd's head as if to say "I'm here too, buddy."

When he was able to speak again, Lloyd said in a small voice,

"I tried to see my mom and sisters a while ago. I went to the train depot in town, waited 'til the freight train slowed down and hopped it. There were other men on there too, Betty; poor, hungry, angry men not even knowin' where they were going but they were Ok. Nobody bothered me or asked me any questions. We were all just along for the ride.

I went all the way to Mitchell, where mom lives now and jumped off at that station. It was kind of scary, but I made it just fine. I didn't have anything for the girls then, but I knew they'd be happy to see me just the same." He paused for a moment.

"I found mother's flat, a small room where all three were staying and knocked on her door. A man came to the door and, Betty, I swear he was in his undershirt. I thought I'd gotten the wrong room, but then I saw my mom standing behind him, just lookin' at me like she didn't know who I was. The man told me to go away. I told him I wanted to see my mom and sisters and he said my sisters weren't there and I couldn't come in, my mom was busy. Then he slammed the door in my face and that's the last time I saw her. I didn't know what to do, Betty, I had no money, no place to stay, nowhere to go, so I went back to the train station and slept that night under the dock.

When the train came through the next day, I jumped on and headed home." He sat in thought for a moment. "I want to see my mom really bad and I think if I brought her a box of candy or some perfume or something, she'd like me again. But you know the Foleys need to stay in their home too, so I gave them all the money I had. Now I will never get to see my family again, ever."

And with that, tears started to roll down his cheeks again.

The men were back up at the house and were making small talk. Nobody really spoke about the baby's death, especially not in front of Etta or the family. It just hung there like the dirt blown in on the wind, bad, hurtful but not a thing anyone could do about it.

Everyone ate something, there seemed to be a lot of food but it was a somber group, even the children were subdued.

Betty came into the parlor with Lloyd. They found a plate and got a little bit to eat. It was a good feeling not to have to think about cooking for a few days. There was enough food for everyone and then some. Etta sat quietly on the couch and once in a while one of the neighbor ladies would come over to her, take her hand and assure her they were there for her. And then they would take their leave, knowing that soon they would see the family again out at the cemetery.

Betty and Lloyd sat down by Thurber to see what his family was about to do.

"What's your plan, Thurber?" Betty asked.

"We are leaving in a few minutes to go back home. I'm really happy we aren't going West. I want to stay here. This is home and I want to be here."

"Good Thurber, we want you to stay too."

Just then, James came in to announce it was time to head back to the homestead. They would be there until the bank auctioned it off. Betty wrapped up some of the food for them, gave them a jar of milk and the six eggs they had collected the night before and said their goodbyes for the time being.

Betty walked Lloyd out to the old bent gate that hung at an angle on a post that had long ago disentangled itself from the fence.

"Lloyd, my Dad needs your help, yours and mine. He won't exactly tell me what his plan is, but he's got something up his sleeve. Are you willing to help us?"

"You know I am Betty, anything your dad wants me to do. You just let me know what and when."

"You need to get back home now, but I will see you tomorrow. At the cemetery."

"Yep, I'll be there. We can talk more then." And with that, Lloyd started walking back to his house, his house of silence, of painful memories of cold, blank walls, almost as if it were his tomb. Lloyd carried a sack of food from the day back to his Dad. It was a peace offering.

Chapter 10

The Cemetery

Daylight came with a vengeance, hot, dusty and very dry. Betty had slept fitfully because it was so hot in the small frame house and her mind raced all night. She could hear her mother and father in the next room talking but could not make out what they were saying. Her brothers, Albert, Christian and Daniel, spent most of the night outside, although there was no relief from the heat out there. Gretta and Willow took their blankets, threw them on the parlor floor and slept there.

Betty drew some water from the cistern and started the fire in the woodstove to boil the water for breakfast. She picked from the food that the neighbors left the day before and it was such a relief not to have to fix much. She was tired.

Alfred came in to see how it was going and to see if there was any coffee leftover from the day before. Betty heated a cup for him and he went into the parlor. Betty fixed her mother a cup of coffee and took it to her. Etta lay there on her bed, eyes open but not moving. It took too much energy and she had just given birth.

"Momma, I brought you a cup of coffee, do you want it?"

"Sure honey, just set it by the bed for now. I'll get it in a minute."

Betty sat the coffee down and stood there for a minute, trying to find words that just would not come to a 12-year-old. Finally,

"Momma, where is Frederick?"

"What do you mean, honey?"

"I mean, Momma, is he in heaven? If we bury him today, will he be scared? Will he be mad at us for leaving him there? Why did God take him? God already has all the angels he needs, he doesn't need another one." For the first time, Betty was feeling her anger.

"Come sit down Betty."

Betty moved to the bed and sat by her mother.

"Here's what I think. He's asleep in God's arms, plain and simple. He's not crying for us, he's not looking down at us wondering why we left him behind, he's asleep. You know when you go to sleep at night you don't remember anything? You don't know if it's midnight or if the wind is blowing or anything that's happening around you, right? Well, I think that's how Frederick is right now; he doesn't know anything, but someday he will and we will be together, all of us again. I don't know where or when, but we were promised that. And when you say God took him to be an angel, I don't think that's really true either, honey. He has too many angels to even count. The Good Book talks about time and unforeseen circumstances. That means things happen that we can't blame God for, I don't think God "took" him. Man has hurt himself, honey. We can't blame God for all the stuff happening to us. Just think about this. God and the angels must be crying right now too, because they love us and don't want to see us unhappy. It hurts them to see this, so we have to take responsibility for a lot of what's happening right now. Trust me, it's going to be OK."

She looked at her daughter, wondering if what she said had any impact on her thoughts, her fears.

" Now, can you hand me that coffee? We need to get ready. We will say our goodbyes to our baby today. Just remember it's not forever."

"OK, Momma, I'll remember," hesitating at first but then as if adding a footnote, "but I'm still very sad."

"I am too, sweetheart, I am so, so sad."

Most of the town folks met at the little Methodist church, a small white building that needed paint but was helpless against the wind and dirt that pummeled it regularly.

People filed in quietly, greeting each other with a nod or a handshake. The ladies wore hats with veils and the men wore their best Sunday suits. It was stifling in the little church with not so much as a wisp of fresh air. The ladies brought hand fans and the men soon took off their jackets and rolled up their sleeves against the heat. Nobody cared, it was too hot.

Brother Jones came to the front of the little church and stood at the pulpit. There stood a tiny wooden casket closed to the world. Betty drew in her breath. She felt claustrophobic for her baby brother, so small and tight was his world now. The sermon was short against the background of the congregation sitting in the huge wooden pews. The members were all restless and it showed.

"Friends, we are here today to lay to rest one of our own, little Frederick Peterson. He never had a chance to know us nor we him, but we love him. He never drew breath here on earth but he will forever be remembered. Someday we will meet him and be together again in a beautiful place with golden streets and beautiful buildings. We will all walk together and meet the Lord in person. In the meantime, we know he's in a better place, a place full of love. He's with Jesus now. Let us pray." And then he said a few words against the fierce whipping of the fans and the rustle of clothes. And Betty's anger was starting to tell on her. How could be buried in the ground be a better place for Frederick?

Didn't the preacher see he was right there in front of him in a tiny wooden box about to be put in a hole in the dirt? Couldn't he see that? "Blind fool" she wanted to yell at him. Betty did not lower her head, she did not pray with the rest of the congregation but held a steady gaze at the little casket.

Behind the church stood a small cemetery. There were grave markers of all those that had gone before, including many children and each marker told a story of sorts. Most were made of wood and had been partially eaten by starving rodents or grasshoppers; some were made of stone engraved with names, dates and sometimes cause of death. All too often, it seemed there had been a mysterious sickness, one nobody had a name for but a sickness everyone usually recognized because of a cough or wheezing or lack of breath.

There was a hole dug already waiting to receive Frederick. They all went out and stood in the blazing sun while Alfred, Albert, Daniel and Lloyd brought the little casket out and placed it by the grave.

The minister said "Lord, receive this child unto you now." And with that, they lowered little Frederick down into the South Dakota dirt, the dry miserable dirt. Alfred and Etta took a handful of dirt and showered his casket, then turned and walked away, with Alfred holding her up as they walked. Etta was tired and needed to rest. The rest of the Peterson children did the same and then walked away, going back to where the truck was parked. But Betty just could not bear to leave him.

She stood there with fists clenched, holding back tears that were on the verge of falling. This was SO unfair. This whole situation, this life they were all enduring, was unimaginable. At this moment, Betty hated all of it. She hated her house that was always full of dust, she hated having to cook all the time, she hated having to draw water from the cistern with rats or bugs in it, she hated watching her mother and father struggle, she hated being sick with epilepsy, but most of all she hated that her new baby brother was dead!

"Come on, Betty, it's time to go." Lloyd had come up behind her and as much as he wanted to comfort her, he knew he couldn't. There was no comforting the grief that held everyone captive.

"Where are we going to go, Lloyd? Just tell me, is there a place for us?"

"Home, Betty, we need to go home now."

"I hate home Lloyd, I hate it." And the tears started.

"I hate my house too, Betty. You know I lost my family, not the way you lost your baby brother, but they're gone too. All I have is Scout and I almost lost him. Your Dad saved him for me and I will be grateful forever to him, but I have to go back to an empty house with a man I don't even know. I don't know what happened to us, but I know I hate it too."

"You know Momma told me I could take care of Frederick.

Mamma gave each of us a baby to care for and he was going to be mine. I had everything planned for us and now it's all gone."

"We did the best we could, Betty. We could do no more. It was just not meant to be. And I am SO sorry."

"What is there left, Lloyd? There's nothin', no way to live, nothin'"

"We're gonna be OK, Betty. I promise, I PROMISE. You wait and see but now time to go home, folks are waiting." Lloyd took Betty's hand and with that, Betty turned her back on her baby brother and together, they walked back to the waiting vehicles.

Chapter 11

The Bank

Several hot dry weeks passed and life went on as usual. The menfolk had to go into town and collect what food and water was available at the time. Lloyd would walk the half-mile or so every morning to take care of Scout and help around the Peterson farm. He loved being there. It seemed so peaceful and orderly and in the midst of all the chaos in his young life, he really needed that. He would get up early, help around his dad's place and then go over to take care of his horse and Scout was still his horse even though he'd sold him to Mr. Peterson. Alfred made him welcome and Lloyd knew he would someday be able to buy Scout back. In the meantime, his best friend was safe. Lloyd felt really good about it.

On one of the days the men were gathering on the street, the banker, Mr. Gordon Whitfield, came around and handed out a flyer. It was an announcement for an absolute auction of the Foley's homestead. There were no restrictions on the price, no reserve so the place would just go to the highest bidder.

Alfred, James along with his son Thurber were standing with some of the other farmers. Banker Whitfield looked at all of them apologetically. The Banker was not a mean-spirited man and he hated this as much as any of them. He had been raised here and knew all of these men, knew they were good folks fallen on hard times but his hands were tied. The main office in Mitchell had spoken and they were the bank gods.

"Does the bank have someone coming in to bid against us, Gordon?"

Gordon Whitfield, the National City Bank manager, stood for a moment, not sure what he should say.

"Yep, Alfred, he's coming in today first thing. I have to go get him at the train station in Kadoka. Then I'll be leaving him at the hotel. Tomorrow I'll be making my way out to the farm. He'll be heading that way too. Sorry, James, I don't want to have to do this. Your family has been here for a long time now."

"I understand, Gordon. And you understand I gotta do what I gotta do."

The banker nodded and with that, he turned and left the group.

Alfred spoke, "James, can I borrow Thurber today for a bit? I'd like to take him out to my place to help with a few chores."

"Sure, Alfred, not a problem. Guess I need to go tell the family it's finally here. Can you bring him along in the morning then?"

"Yep, guess we'll all meet at your place tomorrow. Thurber, come with me, youngster. I need your help now."

Later that afternoon, Alfred called a meeting in the barn with Betty, Lloyd and Thurber. He had a plan to save the Foley's home and he needed the kids' help. It was risky at best and desperate, but these times called for desperate measures. Somehow the kids needed to delay the banker's departure for the farm. He could not be there for the bidding.

"So we all know what we are supposed to do then, right? Any questions?"

Not one of the kids said a word, they knew the plan and knew what was expected of them. After Alfred left, they all took an oath, shook hands and swore to carry out the "plan" to the bitter end and to the best of their ability. Nobody else in the world knew what was going to happen tomorrow when the bank tried to auction off Thurber's home except the three kids and Betty's dad. It was scary and exciting at the same time but it had to be done. It must be done!

The next morning after breakfast which consisted of an egg each, some stale bread and half a glass of milk, the three met back at the barn. Betty pulled up half a bucket of water and brought with her what looked like some old raggedy clothes. Each child found something to wear, including hats for the two boys and a scarf for Betty's hair. They mixed some dirt in the water to make mud and proceeded to paint their faces, not totally but so as to look like dirty ragamuffins and to hide their identity from whomever they encountered in town. There was intrigue in the air and a sense of urgency within each of the children. Lloyd brought Scout around and all three mounted their mighty steed, turned his head towards town and went charging into that hot, dry morning to wage their personal war on the establishment.

When they got to Main Street, they moved around behind the bank. There was a bit of shade there and some protection from prying eyes. The plan had begun. They sat on one of the public benches to see if there was anybody around at this early hour. Most everyone would be out at the Foley's place to see who was going to walk away with the farm. The bank usually sent an individual to bid against those interested in buying the land, although not many were willing to bid on property that was rundown and had little or no chance of bearing crops in this miserable time of drought.

Alfred and all the men were arriving at the farm and the Foleys had again packed up their things and were sitting with the others. The children were playing in the dirt but James and Phyllis sat with eyes closed against a raging sun and sorrow that had no description. This was their land, James, his father, mother and brother came here, claimed the 25 acres and built, homesteaded, busted sod to keep this place. Now for no fault of their own, they were going to lose it. Their hope hung on $37.50, all the money everyone had given Alfred the day after little Frederick died, but they all knew since the bank would be bidding also, it would not be enough.

Betty, Lloyd and Thurber moved to the side of the bank that was across the street from the hotel. They did not have to wait long. A tall, thin man in a grey suit and matching hat soon came out of the hotel. He looked to be middle age, slightly stooped with dark, piercing eyes and a hooked nose.

"DOG SNOT!!" Lloyd whispered, his eyes narrowing to slits of pure hatred.

"What?" whispered Betty back. "What's the matter, Lloyd?"

"That's the piece of dog snot that was at my mother's place. He's the one who wouldn't let me in to see her!"

"Are you sure, Lloyd? How do you know?"

"Oh, I know him anywhere, that sneaky slithering piece of crap."

"Hey, you yelled at me for cussing, now you're doing it."

"I don't care, Betty. You let me take care of him, Betty, just let me at him."

"Remember why we are here, Lloyd. Don't mess it up now."

"I won't, Betty, but I'm gonna enjoy this."

And they watched him cross the dusty street heading for the bank.

Mr. Whitfield, the local banker, said the banker from Mitchell would be in town so that he could get the deed to the Foley place from the lockbox in the bank. The out-of-town banker walked to the front door of the bank, which was closed at the time and found his keys. He unlocked the door and stepped in.

Everything, the "plan" hinged on the idea that the kids could get into the bank. If the stranger locked the door behind him, all was lost. They waited a minute or two and then slipped quietly up to the front door of the bank. What a sight that must have been, the three children, faces smeared with mud wearing worn, almost rags for clothes and hats. Lloyd tried the door quietly and it opened! The bank was closed since everyone would be out at the Foley place, so the only one in there was Mr. You-Know-Who Dog Snot himself.

The three kids looked at each other, nodded and entered quickly into the bank lobby. There was nobody in sight and it was strangely silent and kind of dark with the shades drawn. There was a light coming from the bank vault and that was the kids' target. With great stealth, well as stealthily as the kids could be, they made their way to the huge door that was partially open. Inside the vault stood the tall, grey man, Lloyd's nemesis, looking over some papers. All three kids pushed on the huge, heavy door. As it started to swing shut, the man looked up from the papers he held just in time to see Lloyd.

Lloyd couldn't help himself, he yelled, "This is for Jessamine, you slimeball!" and the vault door swung shut. The man inside leapt for the door, but it clanged shut, locking the man from the bank, the "suiter" that left Lloyd in the cold, Lloyd's mom's violator locked in.

He was yelling, pounding on the vault door! The three kids slipped out of the bank, adrenalin pumping, sweat pouring down white and brown dirty faces. They raced around to the back, jumped on Scout and took off before anyone saw them. He would be there until Mr. Whitfield, the local banker, came back to town to open the bank for the day. That would be after the auction, the absolute auction!

"Lloyd, you're crazy! We're going to get caught now that he knows who you are."

"It'll be Ok, Betty" said Lloyd in a not-so-convincing voice.

All this time, Thurber had been observing the whole mess.

"You two are both crazy. We're ALL going to jail, including our folks now. Your dad just wanted us to make him late, not lock him up. I don't want to die in a four-foot cell!". Thurber could have cried at the thought.

"Stop Thurber," said Lloyd. "I'm gonna take the blame. Nobody's going to jail except me."

"We need to go tell my Dad what happened." Said Betty and with that, they headed out to the Foleys' place to let Alfred know what had just happened at the bank.

Chapter 12

The Auction

There was a crowd standing around the auctioneer. He was just getting ready to start the bidding. Folks were fanning themselves and barely looked at the three kids riding up on that skinny, tired horse. Alfred was standing with the men when he saw the three dirty kids heading towards the barn. He waited anxiously while they put Scout up, took off the rags and hats, wiped themselves down and stepped out into the heat of the day.

Betty walked over to her father, looked him in the eye and said "Done." That was it. There would be no Mr. Banker here to bid against them. Mr. Whitfield, the local banker, kept looking up to see if the banker in grey from the big city, one of the bank gods was coming along. The auction was starting.

"What am I bid now for this fine piece of land and these buildings that consist of a house, an outbuilding, a small barn and a shed?"

Nobody spoke at that moment. They were all looking at Alfred. Mr. Whitfield was starting to pace a bit.

"I'll bid $20." Said Alfred. He started the bidding.

"I got $20, anybody else," as he tried to start the auction in his best auctioneer's chant.

"$25" James bid.

"Come on folks, this land is worth a lot more than that, what am I bid?"

"$30" Alfred spoke up.

"$35" came back James.

"$36," Alfred.

"$37," James.

That was it. Nobody else said a word, not one other person spoke up or bid on James' farm.

The auctioneer tried to up it to no avail. This was an absolute auction which meant there was no minimum on the sale, so finally the gavel came down.

"Sold to Mr. Foley for $37!" With that, James and his family had their farm back, their home, their land that they had fought so hard for. And Mr. Whitfield, the local banker, was secretly glad.

The deed was still at the bank but James got a bill of sale from Mr. Whitfield, so it was a done deal. The farm still belonged to the Foley's and the women and children were already putting the furniture back in the house.

Fred took the three kids up to the barn to see what had transpired.

"OK, kids, what happened today?"

Lloyd spoke first. "Mr. Peterson, when we closed the man in the vault, he saw me. He saw my face. Am I going to be in trouble?"

"Tell him the rest of it, Lloyd!" said Thurber.

"Mr. Peterson, he knows who I am. I got really mad when I saw him. He's my mom's suiter, he's the one that said I couldn't see her, he's the one keeping her to himself. He's mean and nasty and I guess I let my feelings get away from me. I yelled out my mother's name. He knows now."

Alfred put his hand to his mouth as he has always done and thought for a minute.

"You locked him in the vault? Got to talk to Gordon. We'll work it out, Lloyd."

"Sorry, Mr. Peterson, are we in trouble?"

"We'll see Lloyd, we'll see. Is he still locked in the vault?"

"Yes sir, and he's yelling real loud."

"Yep, the big old door got shut just in time and he's still in there, probably still hollering his head off," said Betty, giggling a little at the thought.

"Was he OK?" said Alfred.

"He was fine, Dad, just really upset. He's gonna be okay."

With that, they all walked back up to the house. Everyone was in good spirits. James saw Lloyd and called him over to where he was.

"Lloyd, my place only cost me $37 and we collected $37.50, remember?"

"Yes sir, I remember."

"Well, we won't need your money now so I'm giving it back to you."

And with that, James handed over two shiny quarters to Lloyd. Lloyd stood there for a moment just staring at the beautiful silver money, the money he had earmarked to buy his mother and sisters a box of chocolates, the money he had given up so Thurber's family could get their land back. He couldn't believe his good luck. So many good things had happened to him lately. His horse, his best friend, was safe, he had a job of sorts taking care of Scout, he felt close to a family that accepted him for what he was AND now he had the money to go visit his mother and sisters. How lucky could a fellow be? Oh yeah, except for that banker locked in the vault, his mother's "suiter".

The auctioneer packed up his gear and headed out. Mr. Whitfield stood scratching his head. Had the city banker gotten lost? Was there an accident? Did he make it out of the hotel?

Alfred approached Gordon, not knowing exactly how he was going to explain this.

"Hey Gordon, can I have a word with you?"

"Of course, Alfred, what's going on?"

So Alfred haltingly explained what had transpired, how he had asked the children to somehow waylay the banker until the auction was over. He explained further that they had done a great job, but unfortunately, it meant they locked him in the vault at the bank, which may be interpreted as some sort of kidnapping. He also told Gordon that the banker knew who the children were because of the anguish

Lloyd had gone through at his hands. He told him about Lloyd's outburst at finding out who he was. The two men stood silently for a moment, looking at each other and then Gordon Whitfield burst out laughing. Alfred was totally confused. How was the fact they were all going to jail funny?

"Oh Alfred, this is one for the books!"

"Then can you help us, Gordon? The kids didn't mean it. They just did what they did in the spur of the moment. If anyone's to blame, it's me."

"Alfred, nobody is going to jail, trust me. I need to go free the banker, but nobody is going to be in trouble. That's a promise."

Mr. Whitfield got in his car and headed into town to release the banker. That property had sold for $37 and although he knew now it was some kind of conspiracy, he was not angry. Actually, he was relieved. He didn't want to see any more of the hardworking folks leave, the families he had grown up with. Mr. Whitfield, the banker, smiled to himself and then burst out laughing again.

He got to the bank and realized the front door was unlocked. The street was deserted except for a lazy dog trying to get out of the heat. He stepped inside the building and hollered to see if anyone answered. From the vault came a muffled sound and then someone yelled, "HELP!!"

It was, of course, the Mitchell banker from Central. Mr. Whitfield went to the vault and stood before the massive door. He knew the combination, so he unlocked the big door and swung it open. There stood the city banker, his hat and coat laying on the floor, his bow tie askew and his hair a tangled mess.

"What in the world---?" He acted surprised.

"Rowdy, dirty nasty little brats, that's what. I got a good look at one of 'em and I know him. I am a friend of his mother and will she ever hear from me about this."

"We definitely will do some serious investigating, Ronald. We will have to, of course, talk with your "friend" so she can identify him and then we'll have to discuss this whole situation with the town council and your wife. They will need to understand what transpired here today. And, of course, the bank will need to know how these "children" got the best of you, how the bank was left unlocked."

All of a sudden, the Mitchell banker got a "deer-in-the-headlights" look.

"Well, I'm not certain it was him. It could have been anyone, really. I need to do some research on my own before I let anyone know what went on. It could be I just locked myself in and was seeing things. Yes, that's what it was, I'm sure. I locked myself in the vault. Thanks for getting me out of there. I'm going to go back to the hotel and rest up before heading home. How was the auction?"

"We sold the place for $37."

The Mitchell banker about choked, but his hands were tied, so he bit his tongue and walked back across the street to lick his wounds. Mr. Whitfield deposited the $37 and marked the deed paid in full.

The Foleys would not have to leave their home, Lloyd was safe from the law, Mr. Whitfield, the local banker, was happy and Mr. banker/god was now just praying nothing was ever spoken of again.

Chapter 13

A New Beginning

Everyone left to go home. All were happy at the outcome, especially the Foleys. The folks in the community stuck together and it worked out in everyone's favor.

Lloyd and Betty sat on the porch for a while a little nervous but very exuberant at what had happened that day. They did make a difference and most importantly, Thurber and his family had their farm back. And it was starting to cloud up a bit, not the ugly brown roiling clouds coming in from a distance but a slow darkening of the day. The two kids sat watching the clouds form and they could feel a dampness in the air. It was still hot but there was definitely rain in the forecast. Then a sprinkle! And another sprinkle and the two sat relishing the drops as though they were diamonds falling from the sky.

They sat in silence for a while, letting the droplets of rain wash over them, sticking their tongues out to catch the bounty.

"Betty, I need to tell you something. Just listen to me." Lloyd took a deep breath and said "I'm gonna marry you--"

She interrupted him, "NO Lloyd, no, I'm never getting married! NEVER" and she stood up as if to run away.

"Why not, Betty?" Lloyd was really hurt by her refusal of what he deemed was a proper proposal.

"Because Lloyd, when you get married, you have kids and when you have kids you have heartbreak, you lose them, they go hungry, you can't buy what they need and you can't save 'em, that's why!"

"Betty, listen to me a minute. I'm gonna be famous, I'm gonna be a singer and I'm gonna be rich. I'll buy you anything you want, a nice house with a pond full of water and fish, a place to garden and a yard with grass and trees, fruit trees so we can just go out and pick what we want to eat. I promise Betty, I won't let you down, ever."

He sat silently looking at her, this SMALL, skinny 13 year-old with blond hair and big blue eyes, sad, unhappy eyes. Rain was starting to turn the dust to mud, starting to clean the air around them. For the first time in a long time, Lloyd could smell the damp earth and he knew in his heart he loved Betty and that she would be his one day, not now but one day.

Betty sat looking at Lloyd for a minute and realized he meant it. She had never in all her 12 years had a proposal of marriage and it really threw her off guard. Betty was always very guarded. That was life on the South Dakota prairie, you never once let your guard down, it was too harsh, just the day-to-day living was a challenge. Being a Prairie Child brought challenges every day along with heartaches and pain, real physical pain. She thought about her parents struggling to feed and care for so many with never quite enough and she thought about her baby brother and she knew his tiny little life would be forgotten over the years when all of them were also gone. She thought about Thurber and his family. They certainly weren't out of the woods yet. Hunger was always just around the corner and there never seemed to be an end to this godawful drouth swallowing up everything green and living, leaving nothing but dirt and grasshoppers in its wake.

Her mind wandered to the small town where everyone eked out a living, just barely subsisting, having only neighbors to help. But then she realized there was hope, hope in that band of people who chose to come to the prairie, to build homes and live their lives honestly (well, almost honestly, her mind reenacting the episode of the Banker).

"Betty, did you hear me?"

She had.

"I'll consider it in a few years, Lloyd, if you are that serious. I will think about it. I won't promise, but if I ever DO get married, I will let you know first."

And Lloyd was happy! He had a promise of things to come, he had his horse Scout, a future with his mom and sisters when he could knock on her door with a big box of chocolates in hand, a place he could escape to, Betty's place and maybe, just maybe a partner in life." And life was good.

"What day is it, Betty?"

"I don't know, Lloyd, it's the 13th. I know that, why?"

"We need to remember this day, the 13th, the 13th of summer. I'm gonna marry you on the 13th of summer."

And it started to pour down rain.

Part Two

Black Blizzard, White

Chapter 14

The Hard Facts

Life, on the South Dakota prairie, went on and on and for the next four years Betty, her father Alfred, her mother Etta and the rest of the kids survived the drought that hung on like a sickness. There were spurts of rain just enough to keep the cistern wet. Help had finally come to some of the farming communities in the form of commodities. Once a month, the family would pile in the old pickup truck and head for town to collect their issuance, peanut butter, cheese, canned meat, some flour and a little sugar. The sugar was especially prized and always saved for special occasions. Then there was a war being fought overseas, a war nobody worried too much about because the United States was staying neutral. That would change soon enough.

Betty continued to help her mother around the homestead, doing a lot of the cooking and cleaning. There was always the dust and no matter how hard Betty tried, it never went away.

Alfred had almost given up on planting any crops. They just seemed to wither and die, but Etta was able to keep a small garden growing. She got tomatoes, onions, a few green beans and some peas. The birds were always after those, along with the hoppers and beetles, but she was diligent so she was able to gather a few vegetables. The chickens were essential to the family's well-being. Gathering eggs was critical every morning and a setting hen guaranteed chicks. The Roosters were more in danger as the lesser ones became food. That was just a hard fact of life. The old cow gave them another calf, a female which was great since they were also the life-bread of the farm.

From somewhere out of the blue, a cat showed up, made her home in the barn and had kittens. Where she came from, nobody knew, but she was welcome as she kept the mouse population down. When the boys milked the cow, they would squirt a little milk at her and her babies. She was skinny but happy to have found a place to call her own.

Betty did not go to school regularly. She went when she felt good but she still dealt with epilepsy. It was a disease that was little understood in 1940. It seemed to come on if Betty was nervous or upset, so everyone tried very hard not to bother her. She was beginning to understand her body more and that helped her. If she felt like she might be getting ill, she would excuse herself and try to calm down. It's called "bio-feedback" today.

Living in poverty was a fact of life for her, but despite the drudgery of her everyday routine, she was becoming a young lady. Like all young girls starting to grow up, Betty had her dreams. Her thoughts often went to the pretty dresses pictured in the Ward's catalog, which could be delivered by mail right to her door. She dreamed of fancy underwear made from real silk with matching camisoles and silk stockings held up by a garter belt. She wanted her own brush and comb and a mirror so she could put on a little powder and she loved the thought of having her own luscious, creamy tube of lipstick. She also hoped someday to have her own room, an impossibility with so many kids in the small frame house. But most of all, she dreamed of a romantic love that always just ended with a kiss. Innocence never dreamed of more than that. And she thought about Lloyd.

Lloyd continued to work for Alfred to help feed and care for his horse, Scout. Lloyd saw Betty almost every day, but as he got older, he kept his distance. They were polite to each other when the occasion was called for, but they did not speak of that time so long ago that threw them together. He didn't want to scare her away because he knew someday he would marry her, even if she didn't want to admit it.

He was almost 18 and becoming very independent, having long ago figured out how to move around his father. He did not see his mother again and only recently learned that she had moved cross country to California. She had taken the two girls and drove them all the way cross country in an old Model A. It was his understanding that she had remarried and changed her name. He wasn't sure how to get in touch with her but knew he would see her again someday, someday when he was famous and rich. And he would buy her anything she asked for.

He wanted to learn to play guitar, that was his goal, but first he had to get one. That was the hard part, saving enough to buy a new guitar. He knew he could become a singer, that was his passion.

He had his own dreams too, dreams of going to Nashville, wherever Nashville was, and being "discovered" and making so much money he would never have to worry or be hungry or go without things like shoes ever again and he would provide for Betty who would be his wife. His mother and sisters probably needed his help, as did Alfred and Etta and the Foleys. Lloyd knew if he had money, he'd come back to the community and help all who needed it and that was just about everyone. He always figured he would buy a huge house in California, move his mother and sisters into it along with Betty. Such were the dreams of the child of the prairie.

Chapter 15

November 11th, 1940

"**M**om, the dishes are done, the floor's swept and the bread is rising, can I go now?"

"Where are you going, Betty?" Etta said as she stitched away on a piece of fabric, an old worn shirt that belonged to Alfred and needed mending.

"It's SO nice out today, I want to see if I can get some of those catfish over at Schneider's dam. He says I can fish anytime I want over there."

Etta looked out the back door. It was particularly warm for November. The boys were out by the barn in shirt sleeves and everyone was enjoying the weather, but it didn't seem right to her. Something was in the air.

"Betty, it's almost a mile over there. I just don't trust the weather's going to stay like this. I don't think you should leave right now."

"Mom, please, I can also pick up some cow pies while I'm there. We need fuel for the fire. Our wood's running a little low right now and we won't be getting any more until the end of the month. I won't be very long, I just want to get away for a little while. PLEASE!"

Etta looked out at the clear blue sky and drew in a breath of fresh air which was not heavy with dust for a change.

"OK, baby, but you take a jacket, hear?"

"Oh Mom, it will just weigh me down. I'm going to take a sack and a pole. I'll catch something to put on the hook when I get there."

"Take a jacket, Betty, or you can't go." Etta was firm and Betty knew that was her final word.

Betty gathered up her things, the sack for the "pies", a stringer for any fish she caught, her pole and, OK, a light jacket. She would be home long before dark; it was so nice out she just couldn't understand what the big deal was.

As she left the yard, her brothers called out to her.

"Where are you going, Betty? Can we go?"

"No, Daniel, you can't. I want to be by myself for once."

"Where you going to be by yourself, Betty?"

"Schneider's dam. I'll catch us some catfish for supper." And with that, Betty left the yard and turned her attention to the dirt road that was calling her name.

As she walked down the country road, she felt a promise. The prairie was brown and barren and looked like those old photos her mom kept in a box, Sepia tone it was called although mother's photos turned brown with age. It was unusually warm for November and there were creatures taking advantage of the day along with Betty.

What was the promise that the day held? Betty could feel it in her bones, in her heart, in every breath and it felt good to be promised something, whatever it was. She skipped a little and then remembered she was a "grown-up". Well almost.

After a half-hour, Betty came to the Schneider's gate. The house was long gone, but there was an old pump house sitting by the dam and cows were around the water's edge drinking from it, stepping in the mud, and munching on what dry prairie grass there was. Betty decided to find some bait and drop her hook in the water and then go collect some "pies" if she could find some dry enough. Cow dung actually made pretty good fuel when wood got low.

Betty looked around for some bait and Voila! There sat a robin on a fence post with a worm in its mouth. Betty threw a rock at the bird, which scared her enough that she dropped the worm and flew away.

"Perfect!"

Betty ran and picked up the poor hapless worm and made her way down to the water's edge. It was muddy, the sun having warmed the cold earth around the dam and there were deep depressions where the cattle had stood, but Betty was delighted with her good luck. The Promise!!! It was going to be a great day, just Betty and the worm.

She hooked the wiggly, damp creature on her hook and dropped it in the water. Next, she took the gunny sack she had brought and headed up the hill to find "fuel", dry cow dung.

Schneiders were rich, at least by Betty's estimation. They had about 100 acres of land and about 20 head of cattle. They brought feed in from outside the area and the cows looked healthy. Schneiders owned a butcher shop in town and everyone knew their meat was good.

Sometimes Mrs. Schneider would give away meat scraps and bones to folks. Betty visited the shop when she could and Mrs. Schneider always gave Betty something to take home. It made great soup or stew depending on what was at hand and Betty really appreciated that. Betty wanted to work in the butcher shop selling fine meat, just waiting patiently for the opportunity to be a salesperson. She started collecting her "fuel" while watching the fishing pole.

Alfred came in for lunch after working all morning in the barn, mending harnesses. He heard from the other farmers that 1940 was supposed to be a better year for crops and he was anxious to start over again. After all, he was a farmer.

He was a quiet man, not given to smiling, laughing or small talk, but he was concerned today. As he came in the door, he noticed the wind had picked up slightly and had changed direction. It was now coming out of the Northwest.

"Mother, where are the kids?"

Etta, who had just put away the shirt she was mending, started to heat up the cook stove to fix them a cup of coffee and some soup.

"Christian is in town with Willow. They're getting a few things we need from the grocer. Albert and Daniel were in the barn with you and Gretta is in the bedroom looking at the Christmas catalog. Why? What's wrong?"

Etta knew instantly, having been married to Alfred for so long, that he was concerned about something.

"The wind has changed direction. It's coming out of the North now. Where's Betty?"

"She's over at Schneider's place fishing."

"When did she leave?"

"About two hours ago. Said she needed a break and was going to bring home some fish for dinner. She should be along anytime now." But now, Etta had a look of concern. Betty had been lost once before in a dust storm, a black blizzard, and only saved by the milk cow who knew her way to the barn.

"Betty is smart, she knows if the wind comes up, she needs to head for home." Etta didn't sound very convincing.

They sat at the kitchen table, looking out the back door, hoping to see Betty coming down the dirt road. The wind was picking up and the temperature was beginning to drop. The two younger boys had come in and were in the parlor playing checkers. No Betty. The parents sat drinking a cup of coffee along with a bite of soup and they could see clouds, rain clouds forming to the North. The temperature was now dropping rapidly.

"What did Betty have with her Mother?" Alfred asked, all the while looking to see if Betty was coming down the road.

"She took a sack, her fishing pole and, I hope, a light jacket. I didn't see her leave. Alfred, do we need to go get her? Does the truck run?"

"Christian has the truck in town so I'm gonna hike on over to Schneider's place and bring that girl home. It's getting cold out there. I think we're in for a bad storm."

Alfred was irritated that he had to get out in what was becoming a windy, cold day but he had to find Betty. This was going to be bad and he knew it.

Chapter 16

The Promise

Alfred made his way to the barn to get a few things, his old heavy jacket and one for Betty that belonged to the boys. Etta had pulled a quilt off the bed and rolled up a couple of hats, gloves and some socks, tied it with a belt she had and handed it to Alfred, who slung it over his shoulders. He took a worn rubber raincoat and put it over all of that.

Lloyd was there in the barn taking care of Scout and getting the cows put up. The chicken coop had been secured as best it could be.

"Where you going, Mr. Peterson?"

"Got to go get that scatterbrain Betty off Schneider's farm. She's out there fishin'."

"Let me go with you, Mr. Peterson, I can help. This weather doesn't look good at all."

"No, Lloyd, you stay here with the rest. I'll get Betty and we'll be along shortly."

With that, he was out the barn door and into what was becoming a gale-force wind blowing directly out of the North West. He headed Southeast fighting an ever-increasing wind that was pushing him at his back, trying to knock him down.

Alfred's old pants did little to keep him warm. They were worn thin and his boots were also in bad shape. There was a hole in the bottom of one and already, he could feel the cold, damp weather reaching in like someone trying to take his boot off his foot. He made a note to himself to repair his boots when he got home.

Betty had been successful in catching fish. She had three on the line and another nibbling at what was left of the worm. Her sack of "pies" was full and she wanted just that one more fish. Those old bottom-feeders tasted like the mud they ate and were full of tiny, sharp bones but it was food and she was going to bring it home for her family.

She began to notice the wind and the dropping temperature so she put on the little jacket, thankful now that she had it. The weather was getting worse, but that darn fish kept nibbling at the bait.

"One more, come on, buddy, grab that worm," she thought while starting to hunker down along the bank, staying back from the mud that was now getting a little harder with the dropping temperature. She waited and waited, too long now. Betty never got that last fish and by the time she picked up her gear, it was blowing hard and she could barely see. It was beginning to spit sleet, not rain, just little bits of stinging ice and Betty now realized she might be in trouble.

Needles of ice hit her all over and stung like a thousand bees. She was so intent on catching that last fish Betty had not realized how cold it was becoming or how dark it was getting with the huge clouds rolling in. Her direction for home was West and the storm was blowing in from the Northwest so it was like fighting a tiger in a tank of water. For every two steps she took, she was pushed back by the wind three steps. The huge gunny sack slung over her back didn't help and the light jacket she grabbed on her way out the door did nothing for her. Her option was to go to the only shelter around, the old pump house that was dilapidated and ready to collapse. It had been useful in its day since there had been a working farm close by, but now it lay in ruins, just a shell of what it had been, the rusted machinery and long black conveyor belt lay silent, attesting to destructive powers of Mother Nature.

Was this the promise? Was this the result of the exuberant sense of something happening in her life today? Was this, in fact, a cruel joke played once again on Betty, on her family, on her friends, in this god-forsaken place? How could she have been so stupid, as to believe that the promise she felt this morning, was anything other than another painful lesson in her young life? And how long would the Promise allow her to live? She now felt a foreboding, felt the insult, the slap in the face by the very prairie that gave her life.

"Promise me anything but give me nothing and steal what little I have! GO TO HELL IN A HANDBASKET!"

As she made her way to the pumphouse, she thought she saw a figure coming across the field. The ground was beginning to gather ice and snow, turning white as the wind blew unimpeded across the flat, endless prairie. Someone was headed her way.

Oh God, who could that be? Maybe it's a murderer or a crazy person who just wants to hurt girls, Betty thought, but then she recognized the tall, lanky figure as her father, Alfred.

That was worse! He had to leave the warmth of his kitchen to come out and find her. Betty almost wished it was a "murderer" instead of him.

Alfred reached the pump house about the same time Betty did and both were cold and anxious to get inside. The door had been secured but it didn't take much to break the wooden plank that nailed the entrance shut. Just as they got the door open, they both saw another figure approaching from the West. It was a horse with a rider. LLOYD!!!

"Oh papa, that's Lloyd on Scout. Oh no, he's come after me too." She was in distress at the thought of these two men (yes, she now thought of Lloyd as a man) and that poor horse having to rescue her, but she was also relieved. She now had a chance and she was grateful for that.

When Lloyd got to the door of the pumphouse, they could tell he and Scout were cold too. They all had to get out of this now raging storm, soon to be a South Dakota blizzard. They all knew the hazards of being out in this weather. It was extremely dangerous. Anyone caught out in it would not make it. There had been school children found days later dead, from a blizzard that came up as quickly as this one, and several neighbors in the past had died just going from their house to the barn. It could be and would be brutal.

"Mr. Peterson, I couldn't let you come out here by yourself so I followed you. Darn, it's cold!"

"It's OK, Lloyd, let's try to get Scout in here. At least it's out of the wind."

And with that they pulled the old horse inside the building. It wasn't exactly winterproof and the wind came in all the cracks, but at least the snow and stinging ice didn't hit them.

The old equipment lay silent and sinister and had a lot of debris, including old bird's nests and mouse droppings. The dust was thick from years of non-use, so while Betty wrapped herself in a damp but not really wet blanket, Alfred and Lloyd set out to clear the best spot available to them, behind a huge piece of machinery that gave them some protection from the storm. They scooped out the dirt with their bare hands and hung the rubber overcoat over the openings in the wall. That gave them some protection but it was still very cold. All of them shivered in the now below freezing temperature. It had dropped 30 degrees in a matter of minutes.

And the Blizzard came alive and danced across the prairie like a drunken sailor and raged like a mad man and the three of them huddled together wondering when or if they would ever get to go home again.

Chapter 17

The Blizzard

Alfred started to take stock of what was available to them. There was, of course, the rusted metal parts from an old pump, a long black rubber belt that had broken and lay under the machinery, several other machines that he was unfamiliar with and lots of dead grass from the animals that made their nests in the building.

"Betty, what's in the sack, hon?" Alfred was still looking around.

"Papa, I have a whole sack of cow pies and I have three fish I caught today." Betty was close to tears.

"Well, we can't leave now until the storm passes, hopefully it's a quick-moving one. But I think if we hunker down, we'll be OK."

Alfred started to pick up some of the old metal pieces, looking for something he could use in which to build a fire.

"Here, help me, Lloyd. We need to get this piece of metal closer to the corner where we're gonna be stayin'."

The metal piece Alfred was tugging at was solid, thick and had been a cover for something long gone. It must have been made of pure iron, it was SO heavy.

"OK, Mr. Peterson, but why do we need this old piece of iron over there?" wondered Lloyd.

"Lloyd, son, we need to start a fire, but the good Lord knows we don't want to burn this shack down, so we'll build us a fire pit."

"What about matches? How can we start the fire without matches?"

Alfred pulled several kitchen matches out of his pocket. He had a habit of chewing on the wooden end of those and always had a few handy. The two of them struggled with the heavy metal cover until they got it over behind the other piece of machinery that would be their protection from this monster raising its ugly head.

And Betty said a silent prayer of thanks.

Alfred handed out the things Etta had packed inside the quilt and made everyone as comfortable as possible. Betty put on the heavy jacket and gloves, Lloyd also took a pair of gloves and they wrapped up in the quilt, while Alfred started a fire in the firepit. He used some of Betty's fuel along with some splintered wood he found around the floor.

"Mr. Peterson," asked Lloyd, "why don't you just use some of that grass the varmints brought in to start the fire. Would it be a lot easier?"

"And what would Scout eat then, son?"

What a smart man, Alfred. At the moment, both kids were grateful he was there, but it also seemed he was telling them it was going to be awhile before they could get home. All of a sudden, three fish didn't seem like much.

The small fire was really welcomed while the blizzard roared outside, rattling the very building itself. There were times when Betty wondered what they would do if the building collapsed. They would die. She saw cattle in the fields on her way over and knew it would not be good for them. If there was anyone or anything out in this storm, it would not go well with them either.

Lloyd got up from sitting around the small fire and went to see about Scout. Scout waited patiently by the opening between the back wall and the piece of machinery that was their protection. Lloyd had saddled him up for the ride, so now he took the saddle off Scout's back and shook out the blanket that had been under it. He wrapped it around Scout's shoulders and down his back. It made a fairly warm cover for him. Lloyd was glad now he'd grabbed that one instead of the smaller one. Scout would be OK, at least that's what Lloyd told himself. He brushed Scout off with his hand just to get some of the dampness away from him and Scout waited, knowing Lloyd was there.

There was no light except for the little fire and Alfred knew they had to keep that going so he decided they would take turns watching the fire while the others slept.

"Betty, you need to keep awake, daughter, and feed the fire so it doesn't go out. I'm gonna take a little rest and then I'll relieve you so you can get some sleep. Are you good with that?"

"Yes, papa, I'll be sure and keep the fire going. Lloyd, you need to take a nap too."

And Lloyd and Alfred agreed so they both closed their eyes while Betty kept watch, staying awake because this was her fault and she wasn't going to let anything happen to her heroes.

Betty fed the little flame for about two hours until Alfred awoke. He had been able to rest if fitfully. It was dark now and he thought it must be after 6 p.m., gauging the time he got to the shelter. The wind was still raging and Alfred knew it would be like this all night and maybe into tomorrow. He also knew that the snow would be 6 feet deep in places or deeper and it was going to be a real struggle to get home.

Home. He was sure his family would be OK. There was wood for the stove, some anyway and food in the pantry. He knew the kids would sleep all together in the big parlor by the potbelly stove and he knew his love, his wife Etta, would be just fine, but he was concerned about the two older kids that had gone to town to pick up some things at the store.

And the wind screamed out in its pain, its anger. It was as though if it could not find peace, nothing would and the wind would make sure of that. Nothing would remain as it was.

Alfred took over the watch while Betty crawled under the blanket with Lloyd. They snuggled there, but there were no thoughts of romance, this was all about survival, about making it through this blizzard, this South Dakota blizzard. Their attention was drawn to the howling wind, the snow hitting the building, coming in the cracks, the life and death situation they were in.

Lloyd knew he still loved Betty and he knew, in his heart, they were destined to be together even though if they didn't make it, it might be throughout eternity.

Betty could not sleep and soon she was back sitting with her father and then Lloyd joined them around the pathetic little fire that was all that kept them from that fierce, obscene attack going on outside. Like a living, breathing entity, the storm would stop for a minute, take a deep breath, renew its strength and determination and howl again.

"Papa, I'm so sorry you and Lloyd had to come find me."

"It's OK, honey. We'll be fine, we just need to be patient. It'll die out here pretty soon."

"When Daddy? When can we go home?" Betty was again on the verge of tears.

"Soon, sweetheart, very soon now." But the wind made that statement unconvincing.

Lloyd went to check on Scout. He was cold but OK for the time being. Scout was now a senior but never a nuisance in his old age. He could be stubborn, but he seemed to sense when Lloyd was serious about something and this seemed to be a good time for patience. Lloyd found several discarded birds' nests, shook the dirt off of the grass, made sure that was all that was in there and fed Scout some. They had melted a little snow and he made sure Scout had a drink. Lloyd was hungry but trusted Alfred to know when to fix the catfish Betty caught. Lloyd had been hungry most of his life, so it was not a new feeling but almost a comforting one. Being hungry meant he was alive and gave him some incentive to keep going.

They spent the night wrapped in the blanket, sitting by the fire, making sure it stayed lit.

Chapter 18

Christian and Willow

C hristian Peterson was the firstborn of Alfred and Etta and at 18, he was most like his father. His disposition was quiet yet strong. He never said much and never complained but worked hard on the farm to help his parents and his siblings.

The day started out warm, really warm for November and all of the kids were running around in shirtsleeves. The girls, including Willow, were in plain cotton dresses, having removed their old black stockings and high ankle boots. What a relief to be shed of those itchy, scratchy old wool leggings if only for a short while.

His father had asked him to drive the mile and a half to town that morning to pick up some supplies. Christian was always happy to oblige since he got to take the truck and visit some of the townfolk. That particular morning Willow wanted to go with him. She had some cream to sell at the Creamery/Locker plant for her mother and Willow LOVED to shop at the local drug store. It was window shopping, but she would carefully plan out everything she was going to buy someday, even down to the price of each item. She could "sample" a little perfume from tiny bottles, check out all the cosmetics and look at the newest hairdos in Hollywood magazines. Willow was becoming a beautiful young lady with blond hair and long, sensuous eyelashes. Her eyes were dark brown like her father, but she had her mother's olive complexion.

She and Christian piled into the truck and after much moaning and groaning from the engine and cajoling from him, it started and they were on their way.

The dirt road was bumpy and rutted, but the kids had been down it a hundred times, so they knew every bump, every hole. It was an adventure holding the cream that Etta had saved after separating it from the milk. Not one drop should be wasted. It was liquid white gold to the family and that quart of cream was worth almost a dollar at the local Locker Plant.

That was their first stop and Willow carefully took the old metal can in to be weighed and inspected.

Jonathan Kruse, Johnny was behind the counter and Willow turned ten shades of red. She felt faint and her heart was beating out of her chest because Johnny was the most handsome boy in town and he flirted with her, a LOT. He liked her and she was head-over-heels crazy about him but then, so were all the girls in the county.

"I, I, I brought some cream to sell."

That was all she could say. She was wishing now she had dressed a little nicer and combed her hair and maybe put on a little powder. She just knew her nose was shiny. Oh great, a shiny nose! She turned to mush whenever she was around him.

"I'll take it and get it weighed, Willow. You sure look pretty today, like you been out getting a little sun."

Oh Lord, it was because she was blushing so bad.

Johnny came back with .97 cents and her empty can.

"You going to the dance on Saturday night, Willow?"

"I expect so, Johnny." Why couldn't she say anything clever like Virginia did? Why couldn't she flirt back? He was the most eligible, most good-looking boy in the county and he was flirting but she knew she would give away her feelings if she said anything more.

"Well, I'll see you there. Maybe we could dance a dance or two."

"Maybe" and with that, she grabbed the money and ran out the door. Where was that worthless brother of hers? He was friends with Johnny. He could have intervened on her behalf.

They spent the whole morning shopping, visiting the stores, stopping at the Five and Dime, the drug store, the Gambles store and finally, the grocer. Willow had to pick up a couple of things there, an onion, some coffee and a bag of salt.

"That's $1.05, Willow," said the kindly old gentleman who ran the grocery store, Mr. Robbins.

"Oh dear, Mr. Robbins, I don't have that much, I need to put something back."

"How much do you have today, Willow?"

"I have .97 cents."

"Well, you just take this stuff and bring me the rest next time you're in town."

"I appreciate that, Mr. Robbins. Thank you and I won't forget."

With that, Christian and Willow climbed in the pickup and headed toward home. It was clouding up and the wind was starting to blow. The temperature was dropping quickly and they were not prepared for cold weather.

About a half-mile out of town, it started snowing and visibility was becoming bad. Christian now had to try and follow the dirt road by memory while trying to miss the ruts. Willow took the old blanket that Etta had thrown over the back of the torn and worn bench seat and wrapped it around herself. It did little to keep out the wind which was whistling through the truck. She looked at Christian, calm, collected, quiet Christian and she could see apprehension growing in him and she knew they were in trouble.

They were about a quarter-mile from home with visibility near zero, the wind blowing straight out of the Northwest. That's when the truck slipped off the road and wound up in a ditch.

They lurched to a halt and while Willow sat quietly, Christian got out to see what he could do. Climbing back in the truck, he tried rocking it out of the ditch but to no avail.

"We'll have to try and get home, Willow. We're gonna have to walk."

"Christian, NO! We can't get out in this stuff, you know that. We'll get lost for sure."

"We got no choice, Willow." With that, Christian, who was already cold, climbed out of the cab of the truck and held the door open for Willow. She did not budge.

"I won't go, Christian. Please stay here. Someone will come looking for us."

"Willow, the drifts are going to cover this truck. We're only about a quarter-mile from home. We need to go now while we still can."

"I can't, Christian." That's all she would say. She turned her back on Christian and curled up in the old blanket.

"OK, Willow, I'm going to go get help. You stay with the truck. I'll be back for you."

And with that, he was gone.

The wind howled and seemed to change direction from time to time. It must have blown between 40 and 50 mph. Willow shook violently as late afternoon descended on the prairie and her feet were numb, along with her hands and face. Christian may have made it home, maybe not, but she knew this was no place for humans nor creatures to be right now.

Willow started to feel a sense of calm, a warm sensation coming over her and she thought it was not so bad after all. She quit shaking and was starting to feel warmer. She had been out there in the truck for what seemed like an eternity, but it really didn't matter anymore. Then she heard a voice at first, only a muffled sound coming from somewhere in the storm, but it got clearer and closer. Then she realized it was Johnny and he was calling her name! She opened the door for him. And the wind howled and screamed.

"Johnny, is that you?"

"Yes, Willow, it's me, Johnny. Boy, you are the prettiest girl here. Can I have this dance now?"

"I thought you'd never ask, Johnny, of course you may. Should I take off my shoes? They're brand new, I just ordered them from the Wards catalogue."

"You do whatever you want to do, sweet girl. Come dance with me before the music ends."

She stepped out of the truck barefoot and she danced in the arms of her sweetheart to Frank Sinatra singing "I'll Never Smile Again". He held her tightly and they danced like there was no tomorrow and she was warm in his embrace, this young girl of 17 just beginning her life, this South Dakota prairie girl. And the prairie denied tomorrow as it was want to do.

Christian did not get far. He had on a light jacket, which quickly became ice-coated. He was fighting the wind as it whipped him like a rag doll so he decided to turn back to the truck, wherever the truck was. He did what he thought was a 180-degree turn going by the direction of the wind, but the wind was fickle and played games with him. It changed direction periodically and it was not long before Christian lost all sense of direction and could go no further.

He could not find the truck, which by now was his only hope. Tears froze to his face because he knew what a desperate situation he was in and there was nothing left but to cry. He fell face first in the accumulating snow, trying to get up once or twice. He called out to Willow, hoping she and the truck were close by. He couldn't know if she heard him nor could he know how close he was.

Thoughts about his life on the farm came rushing to mind as he lay there now in deepening drifts. What the heck, he had a loving family, and he sensed their presence. Then they were there, gathered around him to protect him as they always had. He needed to have his family near him. He burrowed in the accumulating snow drift and it was a haven for him from the howling wind.

There was his father, Alfred, tall, thin but with an inner strength that Christian had always admired and emulated. He saw his mother, Etta, sweet, long suffering, the rock of the family and his brothers and sisters. His mom was holding his tiny baby brother and they were smiling. They were saying it's OK, it will be just fine son. We will be here, and we all love you, Christian. And with that, he closed his eyes against the white darkness.

Chapter 19

The Aftermath

lfred fixed the fish the next morning and they each ate one. He melted some snow, and they all had a drink, including Scout. They spent the morning talking about things past, present and future. Lloyd told about how he had tried to see his mother and sisters but was turned away by none other than Mr. banker man, the banker that had wanted to foreclose on the Foley's homestead. They had a good laugh over that and made a game of pick-up sticks with small sticks that the kids collected around the old building.

The sun came out finally at about 11:00 a.m. and it shone so brightly on the unbroken snowy expanse that it hurt their eyes. It was still bitter cold but the wind had died. They had weathered a blizzard and on the South Dakota prairie, that was a miracle.

"Papa, do you think we can go home now?"

"I don't know, Betty. We need to see how deep the snow is."

And with that, Alfred stood up and headed to the wooden door. Opening the door, he was greeted by a solid wall of snow blocking their exit. Alfred thought for a minute and decided the only way out was to dig out, so he started looking for something to use as a shovel.

He came across an iron bar that he thought might work and Lloyd had a penknife that he used to chop the solid bank of show. Betty found an old iron lid off some unknown piece of machinery and the three started digging a path through the snow piled up against the pump house door. After several hours and little gained, the three stopped to assess their situation again.

Each had taken turns to make certain the fire did not go out and had taken a break now and then. Lloyd always checked on Scout, who stood quietly, that once proud horse, now older, wiser and more subdued.

It was hard work since the snow had been packed by 50 miles per hour winds. Scout was becoming restless. After all, he had been in this building for almost 24 hours, and he was getting anxious. Lloyd went to check on him again and that's when he saw it! The building in the corner had caught fire and it was beginning to crackle with the sound of wet timber trying to burn!

"FIRE!" Lloyd yelled.

Alfred and Betty turned to see a finger of flames starting up the back wall. Grabbing snow they had dug out with their hands, they ran back and forth, throwing it into the flames. Lloyd started lobbing snowballs, but it did little good since the wood was old and dry, the fire was only slowed by the dampness of the snow outside. They were trapped and even though the wood was damp from the snow, the fire was beginning to get out of hand. Scout had sounded the warning and now he was beginning to stomp and whinny, knowing all too well there was danger close by.

The three frantically worked at putting the fire out, running back and forth with handfuls of snow. Alfred grabbed the old blanket and beat the flames to no avail. Scout started kicking and panic was on everyone's faces. They were trapped!

Just as the back wall exploded in flame, Scout kicked the wall he was close to with his hind legs and put a hole right through it and there was daylight. There was little time to lose, the fire was spreading. The three ran to the spot and began tearing at the wood. The snow had not accumulated on the backside of the shed and they could see the unbroken white expanse of the prairie.

Frantic now, they pulled the rotten wood away and when there was a hole big enough for all, including Scout, they made their escape. And just in time, the building burst into flames and it seemed a matter of a few minutes and it was on the ground.

Now there was no choice but to head for home. The snow was deep but not unmanageable. Alfred put Betty on Scout and he and Lloyd trekked ahead to clear a path. Sometimes the snow was up to their waist, sometimes almost bare ground where the wind had blown it away. It was cold!

Alfred knew they had to get home in a hurry or the would-be rescuers would find them in a few days frozen stiff. He knew nothing of his two older children, but in the back of his mind, he was worried. He had a concern for his family back at the farm too. He knew Etta was capable, but he wasn't sure how much wood they had and how much food was available. He was anxious to get home.

It seemed forever out in the middle of nowhere, nothing for miles except white, glistening snow, but the sun was out so Alfred could tell the direction they needed to go while behind them was a plume of smoke still rising against a clear, blue sky. There were large humps covered by snow and they all knew what they were, cattle. Cattle had been out in this stuff and had not survived.

They headed West towards home not thinking about those poor cows or that it might have been them. They were all very cold, but when they came up over the ridge, they saw the house and there was smoke coming from the kitchen chimney! A more beautiful sight there never was. It renewed their energy as they saw salvation close at hand. Warmth! Food! Family! They dragged, pulled and pushed Scout down the slight incline and what seemed like an eternity soon became a reality. Lloyd ran Scout into the barn and removed the wet, snowy blanket. Scout was cold too, so Lloyd brushed him down and found another warm blanket to cover him. After all, he had saved the day. He found some hay and promised his friend he'd be back soon. Scout was content.

Betty and Alfred stepped inside to a warm, inviting kitchen, one they had been in a thousand times before but today seemed especially beautiful. And as they started peeling off cold, frozen clothes, Etta came in. She was SO happy to see them, she cried. Running to meet them, she hugged both and couldn't believe her eyes. They were home, they were safe. At that moment, Lloyd popped in the door, cold, shivering.

Then Etta looked at Alfred and apprehension slowly began to etch her face.

"Have you seen Christian and Willow?"

"They're not here?"

Her voice was almost a whisper, "no."

Betty and Lloyd stopped what they were doing and all were silent for a minute.

"They probably spent the night in town." Alfred was trying to convince himself more than anyone else.

"Does the phone work, mama?" Betty asked. The phone was on a party-line with three other customers and when you rang up, an operator answered and more likely than not, all the neighbors were listening to your conversation.

"I don't know, Betty, we need to try it." And with that, Etta went to the wall phone and cranked it up. No answer. The lines must all be down and there was no telling how long they would be inoperable. Sometimes it was weeks.

Etta made some coffee and the four of them sat around the clawfoot table in the parlor near the potbelly stove. They were all exhausted from the ordeal, but there was a sense of urgency in their voices.

Finally, Betty said what was on all their minds, "What if Christian and Willow aren't in town? What if they're out there somewhere? What if they're in the truck somewhere between here and town, waiting to be rescued? What if---?"

"Betty, honey, we'll go find the kids as soon as we can. Don't you worry. Christian has a good head on his shoulders. They are probably staying somewhere in town until it's safe to come home. I'm sure they're just fine."

Etta's voice cracked a little as she spoke, which gave her true feelings away. To be out in a true blizzard such as this was not only dangerous but lethal.

The late afternoon and evening were spent trying to dig out. Just shoveling a path from the house to the barn took hours. The snow had piled up on the backside of the house clear to the roof and was waist-deep almost everywhere else. The cow and her daughter were in the barn with Scout so they were OK, the chickens, on the other hand, might be in jeopardy.

The three younger children had busied themselves with games during the storm and tried the radio to no avail. Gretta was working on her sewing project and the two boys were playing cards with an old deck that was missing a Jack.

That night the whole family spent fitfully up and down, checking the stove, looking out the window towards town hoping to see lights, listening in the dark for the door to open, for Willow and Christian to come walking in. Nothing.

Early in the morning as they sat waiting, the phone rang! Everyone jumped a mile and Etta, Alfred, Betty and Lloyd all ran to it. Alfred picked it up.

It was Johnny from the Locker Plant in Town.

"Mr. Peterson, this is Johnny, is Willow home?"

"No, Johnny, do you know where they stayed last night?"

"Mr. Peterson, I saw them leave town just as it was beginning to snow yesterday. They were headed home. They aren't home?"

"No, Johnny, they're not. Can you get the firetruck out of the barn? Is there anyone in town to help look for my kids?"

"I'll find men, Mr. Peterson, and we'll be coming your way. Can you get out?"

Just then, Phyllis Foley broke in. She had been listening on the party line.

"Alfred, this is Phyllis, I heard it and James is getting his stuff on to go out looking. He'll meet you on the road to town. We'll find 'em."

"Thanks, Phyllis. I'm gonna crank up the Farmall and try to get out. How about James, can he get out yet?"

"He's got his old John Deere. He says he can push a house with that thing. He'll meet ya at the fork in the road."

Johnny broke in. "I'm on my way now too. Gonna get the men to pull the firetruck out. We're on our way. Don't worry."

But they all were.

Chapter 20

At the End of the Road

Betty was getting her boots and coat on. Lloyd was looking around for anything he could wear and found some things hanging beside the kitchen door just as Alfred and Etta were walking in from the parlor. Betty came in after them, ready to go out in the bitter cold to look for her brother and sister.

"You two aren't going." said Alfred in his most stern voice.

"Papa, I have to go, I have to!" Betty put on her most determined look and stood defiantly in the way of the wooden back door.

"Me too. Mr. Peterson, you need help. I'll dig us out if I have to."

"No, kids, not this time." And with that, Alfred walked past Betty out into the vast white expanse of the South Dakota prairie.

Betty and Lloyd stood looking at each other for a minute and both knew exactly what the other was thinking. They sat at the kitchen table, still fully dressed in their winter clothes, just waiting. Etta moved to the parlor to be with her other children and sit in silence, not wanting to know what she would soon learn. They heard the Farmall tractor start up. Kerchug, kerchug, the engine huffed and puffed until it knew it had to get moving and so it did. It had big metal wheels on the back with spikes all around, so it had traction. The front wheels were also of metal but smaller. Alfred knew he could make it, he knew he had to.

Betty and Lloyd quietly left the warmth of the old kitchen and headed to the barn where Scout was tied. They put a blanket on him first and then the saddle that hung in one of the stalls, long forgotten, the leather stiff with cold and old age. Lloyd's fingers were stiff with the cold too and he had trouble cinching up the straps. Scout didn't like a saddle and thought he should have the last word but to no avail.

The kids found strips of old cloth used for binding and wrapped them around Scout's legs to help keep him warm. They again used the blinders that had lain for so long in a corner, a reminder of another storm, another time, the black blizzard.

The snow was high in places but had blown almost to the bare frozen ground in others so when they left the barn, they tried to stay out of the huge drifts that dotted the bright landscape. It was almost blinding and they dared not look directly at the snow for long.

It took an hour for Alfred to get a short distance to the crossroad where James was waiting with his tractor.

James was a good friend and Alfred was glad for his help. Alfred knew he could find his way but what he couldn't stand was what might be at the end of the road.

James jumped down off his tractor.

"We'll find 'em, Alfred and I think they'll be just fine. Christian is smart and Willow is down-to-earth." But he knew the consequences of being caught out in a storm. It did not bode well for the children.

They followed the road by way of the telephone poles which came directly from town. The tractors chugged along, bogging down every now and then, in which case the men would pull each other out by a strap James had. It was slow going and Alfred was very anxious.

Johnny had alerted several of the men in town, including the old Doctor. He didn't practice much anymore, only tending to emergencies, so the town folk went to the bigger city for their healthcare. They pulled out the old red firetruck and, after several tries, got it started. They drove in the direction the kids had gone the day before, hoping for the best, knowing in their hearts the worst.

Betty and Lloyd had a fairly straight shot into town, not having to stick to a road. When they got about a quarter of a mile from the house,

Betty noticed a glint of something that was covered in snow. As the kids got closer, they realized it was part of a bumper of a vehicle. Betty drew in her breath. Lloyd yelled into the distance.

"HELLO! ANYBODY THERE? HELLO, WILLOW, CHRISTIAN ARE YOU THERE?"

It was so quiet, the sunlight bounced off the ice-bound truck. The sky was a clear blue and exquisitely beautiful. A bird flying high overhead on his way to warmer places called out too, but there was not a breath of life anywhere to be seen. And Betty knew.

Standing totally still, they could hear the sound of the tractors in the distance and then the noise of the firetruck coming from the opposite direction. They dismounted Scout and walked towards the truck half-buried in a drift.

"Betty, honey, you need to wait here, I'll check first."

And for the first time, Betty listened to Lloyd. She stood still and watched as he moved to the truck, cleared off the snow and moved around to the open door. There was nothing in there.

"Betty, they aren't in the truck."

Those words ran down her spine like the ice on the windows. She ran to where Lloyd was standing and looked in. On the floorboard, she saw the coffee and things Willow had bought at the store in town, she saw the old blanket laying on the seat and there on the floor were Willow's new shoes. Willow's shoes.

Betty looked at Lloyd and she could say nothing, neither could Lloyd. About that time, the tractors came into view and from the other way, the sound of the firetruck was getting closer. Scout was pawing the ground, looking for some kind of vegetation under the frozen piles.

"HELLO", Alfred hollered over the din of the Farmall. At first, he thought that Betty and Lloyd were Willow and Christian. It was not until he got closer he saw who was standing by the truck.

"What are you two doing here?" he said as he jumped off the tractor.

"Sorry Dad we had to help. Dad, Willow's shoes are in the truck, just her shoes."

Reality hit Betty and she started to cry. Alfred and James made their way to the vehicle just as the firetruck got there.

As the men gathered around, some started digging in drifts that had piled up across the prairie. It didn't take long. Willow was a few feet from the truck. Her hair stuck to her face as she lay on her side, curled up in a fetal position. There was no life in her, she was gone. As Betty, Lloyd, Alfred and the rest gathered around, Dr. Hoyt bent down to find anything that might bring comfort to the family. She looked like a glass doll, a porcelain doll beautiful in her death.

Christian was discovered just a few feet away, face down, arms outstretched. He must have been trying to reach the truck. Neither of them had been prepared to be out in this disaster, this demon of a storm, this lying, evil tempest that just a few days ago had promised a warm and gentle day. Lying Bitch!

Alfred knelt down by his little girl as if to say "I'm here, honey, and you are safe. God has wrapped his big, warm arms around you."

He then walked over to where Christian lay as if sleeping. Again, he knelt down and took his son's cold, stiff hand.

"I'm here, Christian, too late but I'm here. You are my firstborn, my son, who I put my hopes on. "Rest for now, young man. I will miss you."

Alfred stopped short of telling them how much he loved them nor did he shed a tear because that just wasn't done on the prairie. If you were a man, you buried your babies and moved on, working hard to support the other children that did survive. That was Alfred's lot in life, his whole existence.

The other men gave him space and stood quietly by while he said his farewells. Betty came over to Willow and tried to brush the hair away. It was frozen in ringlets around her face.

"Oh Willow, my dear sweet sister, I love you so much. I will miss you forever. Mom says it's promised to us, so I will be anxiously waiting for you and Christian and our baby brother Frederick."

Betty bent down and kissed her sister's hair. She then moved over to where her father was kneeling by Christian.

"I love you too, big brother." And she cried silently, holding her father's hand. Johnny and some of the others came over and helped Betty and Alfred back on the tractor. Betty took Willow's shoes and placed them inside her coat. She would never again let those shoes go or be left out in the cold. Lloyd followed Scout and James along with Dr. Hoyt followed them home on James' tractor. Johnny and the other men were left to remove the children and take them back to town. The truck would stay until it could be retrieved by someone, usually neighbors that would want to help all they could.

After all, this was the South Dakota prairie and folks stuck together.

As soon as they walked in the door, Etta knew. She leaned against the big oak table for support while her other children watched helplessly.

"We found them, dear." Was all Alfred could say and Etta just nodded her head. The rest of the day was a blur for everyone and Betty just sat by the fire warming Willow's shoes.

That night was the worst night of all for the Peterson family. After James and Dr. Hoyt left, they all just sat in silence. The other children went on into bed but Betty, Etta and Alfred could not sleep. Each of them in their silence, contemplated what they did wrong, how they could have, should have saved the children.

Etta thought she should not have wanted that coffee, Alfred thought he should have made them stay to help with chores and Betty, well, Betty knew that if she had not gone fishing, her father would have gone looking for the kids and been able to save them. None of it was true, of course, but guilt is always with the survivors. It's like a long, lost relative that comes to visit and just hangs around not doing anything constructive. It's just there.

In the early morning hours of the next day, Alfred stood up and started getting his coat and hat on.

"Where are you going, Father?" Betty asked.

"I need to tend to the animals, honey."

"I can do it, Daddy, I'll take care of them."

"NO, stay with mama, I will be back shortly." And with that, he stepped out the back heading for the barn.

Chapter 21

The Silent Scream

Alfred made his way to the barn and stepped inside. It was cold but not bitterly cold like the outside world. He stood quietly for a moment, trying to feel what it might have been like for his children.

Were they shivering, were they in pain, were they calling out for him?

It was then that he fell to his knees, lifted his arms to the sky, threw his head back and silently screamed. And the tears flowed and the silent scream went on and on. He was SO angry, so hurt, so sad and he wondered what he had done to make God so mad at him. He had tried to be a good person, he worked hard for his family, he loved his children but didn't understand how this could happen. Then he had kind of an epiphany. He thought of Job, who lost everything, and it was as though he got a direct answer. As with Job, it was not God who did this but some evil force of nature, some unimaginable sequence of events that took his children. He could not blame God for all of this and he need not blame himself. "Unforeseen circumstances, isn't that what the Good Book says? But why now? Why, in the midst of all of the turmoil, should this happen?" And he silently screamed again. He fell face-first in the dirt and sobbed until there was no more in him.

And then he stood up, wiped away the tears, put aside the pain, the anguish and slowly walked back to the house to comfort Etta, his other kids and especially Betty, his little Betty for whom he had to be strong. And he knew he could be and had to be just like Job, who endured what this old world threw at him. He had to do that for them. He had to fight the elements. Mother Nature was nasty, but he couldn't let her win.

Lloyd sat in the corner of the barn with Scout watching Alfred's anguish and just stayed quiet, not wanting him to know that he was there. It was so personal, so agonizing Lloyd would not have intruded if he wanted to. He saw a side of Alfred he had never seen before, but then Lloyd realized something amazing about these strong, silent men of the prairie. And his own father came to mind, Lucas, who was so stoic, so introspective. 'Could it be his father had these emotions? Could it be losing his mother and sisters had this same effect on him? Is that why he could not talk to Lloyd? Is that why he seemed so distant?' Lloyd thought, "My God, they cry."

Then Lloyd, who seldom if ever shed a tear, who always took his cue from his father, started to cry himself. He cried not so much for himself but for everything these folks endured, for all the suffering he saw, for just being human, for the fortitude of these prairie men. And crying felt good.

Chapter 22

After All is Said and Done

Others lost their lives in the blizzard. There had been a large group of duck hunters from other areas out in the weather. They stood no chance against a raging storm that blew their tents down, killed their fires and took their lives. Their families wanted them home and so, with great difficulty, the wooden caskets were transported by train to their final destinations.

The poor old town drunk, George, was found out behind the Post Office huddled in a corner, a bottle in his hands. He had been waiting for someone to let him in as they were wont to do, but there was nobody there that day, so poor George froze to death doing what George always did.

And then there was Miss Merkle, the schoolteacher. She had gone to school that day even though it was a holiday and school was not in session. She had some paperwork to do and decided to return home when the weather turned on her. She never made it home; her car missed the road and wound up in a ditch. She was loved by her students and devoted her life to them, no she gave her life to them, for them.

It was a hard task trying to dig graves in the cold, hard ground of South Dakota, but many of the town's folks came together and with much sweat and, yes, a little swearing, they dug two graves for Christian and Willow right next to their baby brother Frederick. The day dawned cold but cloudless when they came together to say goodbye.

They were all there and had done a potluck in the church basement. There was lots of food, lots of talk and lots of love. This community knew hardship, knew suffering, so looked Mr. Death in the eye again and came together to protect their own. They formed an emotional barrier around the family.

Alfred and Etta stood by the two simple wooden caskets, Alfred shaking his neighbor's hands, Etta hugging each and every person in line that came out to bid them farewell. Betty stood off from the group by herself, numb with the thought she would never again see her pretty sister thumbing through the Ward's catalog marking everything she planned on getting, or her oldest brother, who always watched out for her, even helping her with her chores. It was Christian that always took care of Betty when she had an epileptic seizure. He would sit by her on the bed, get a washrag for her head and let her know she was Ok.

Johnny came over and sat quietly next to Betty until she acknowledged his presence.

"Hi Johnny, how are you?"

"I'm OK, Betty. I want you to know something. It's just between you and me, OK?"

"Sure, Johnny, what is it?"

"I really, really liked Willow."

"Everybody did, Johnny."

"No, I mean really liked her. I was going to dance with her on Saturday night and maybe I thought I'd ask her out. I wanted to get to know her. I wanted her to be my girl, Betty." And with that, he looked down at his hands which were shaking.

"I am so sorry, Betty."

Betty took his hand and made him look at her.

"Willow would have said yes, Johnny. You were the cat's meow to her and you were all she ever talked about. Frankly, I got a little sick of hearing about you all the time. She thought you were too popular for her, you know all the girls in the county chasing you so she never said anything to you, but I know she would have been so happy. I miss her, Johnny."

And tears welled up in Betty's eyes.

Lloyd came over to the two and eyed Johnny with a little jealous suspicion. After all, Lloyd knew his reputation in the county and considered his competition.

"Hey guys, what's up?"

Betty glanced up and quickly removed her hand from Johnny's.

"Hey Lloyd, come join us. We were just talking about Willow and how much we miss her."

"Hey Johnny. " Lloyd squatted down in front of the two sitting on a bench.

Johnny fell silent for a moment contemplating what he was about to say.

"I joined the Navy and I got my papers. Going to see the world."

"Wow Johnny, that's great but why now? Don't you have school to finish?"

"Naw, I'll do that later. I just need to move on, find some adventure, some life out there. I know it's out there, I just need to make the first move. Betty, can I write to you? I really don't have too many people I want to talk to, but you and I have something in common. Would it be OK?"

"Sure Johnny, you write me and I will write you back ASAP. Promise!"

And Lloyd fumed. Betty was his girl---forever.

And with that, Johnny was gone. Just as Willow and Christian had been in their lives but were pulled away, so was another of the South Dakota Prairie kids.

1941, THE NEXT YEAR
Johnny's Letter to Betty.

Dear Betty,

Sorry I didn't write you sooner. Boot camp was OK and now I'm ready to see the world.

And boy, is there a lot to see! I was assigned to one heck of a ship and we were sent to, of all places, Hawaii!!!! I can't believe my luck. The days are beautiful, the nights are even better. The only thing missing is more girls. Don't misunderstand me, the ones here are beautiful, just too many of us sailors. Haha

I did meet a girl the other night and, believe it or not, Betty, her name is Willow. She's sweet and reminds me of our Willow and I will try to send a picture when I can.

That's about all. Our days are busy but a little boring. Tonight is Saturday night and I've got it off, so me and some buddies are heading to town. Maybe I'll see Willow there. I have to be on board tomorrow, Sunday, as this old tub needs a good cleaning. My ship's name is the Arizona and she's really a beautiful ship. Write when you can. I miss the prairie and all my friends. Tell everyone hello for me. Gotta go and get this in the mail.

Hope to see you in the summer.

Love,

Johnny

Dec. 6, 1941

P.S. tell Lloyd I said he needs to join. Haha"

There were so many conflicting reports in those first days after Japan bombed Pearl Harbor. President Roosevelt declared war on Japan that day. Except for the declaration of war from the United States, nobody really knew what to think or what to expect. Betty never heard from Johnny again. He was killed when the Japanese bombed Pearl Harbor and she never knew if he got to dance with that Willow, but Betty knew she would never dance again. It was too painful.

Just three days later, Germany declared war on the United States so it was official. Lloyd came over, as usual, to take care of Scout. Scout was getting old and Lloyd didn't ride him anymore. Lloyd knew that one day he would have to do the kind thing for his best friend but it was good for now, well for now. After all, spring was on its way and about to show off her moves with spectacular wild flowers. The rains had somewhat returned, so it promised to be a good year. That meant crops again and this old prairie would show the world what it could do. Lloyd was in the barn when Betty came in!

"Hey Lloyd, what's up?"

"I got my draft notice, Betty. I'm supposed to report in a few weeks for induction."

There was a great silence, an awkward silence then between the two because they both knew what was coming.

Lloyd cleared his throat, "Betty, will you marry me? I mean before I go off to war."

The silence was deafening and then Betty spoke.

"Well, I could do worse, Lloyd Arthur. I just don't know, though if I could put up with you."

"I'd be good to you, Betty, I'd do good, honest and like I said I'm gonna buy you a nice home, a car, jewelry, anything you want when I get back. I've always loved you, Betty, since we were kids, you know that. How about it? Will you?"

"OK then. I accept your proposal for marriage, but we have to Ok it with my parents, I am only seventeen and I'm not sure what they will say. They really like you, but we need their OK.

You may kiss me now, Lloyd."

That was her first kiss, this little spunky South Dakota girl, and although Lloyd had kissed Virginia at a dance one night, it was also his first real kiss.

Even though there was war in the air, it was a good time to be alive. Lloyd felt a new beginning. He was going to be a man now with a wife (hopefully) and responsibilities and duty he felt to defend his homeland. That was huge for a young man.

Betty was going to be his bride and he knew she was perfect for him. Where he was more the dreamer, she was focused and down to earth. She would keep him grounded.

There would always be storms, but they didn't last and the sun always came out. Like those storms, the suffering these people endured didn't last and the rewards were immeasurable. Like the sun, hope always shines.

Part Three

East of summer

Chapter 23

East of Summer

Lloyd stood on Main Street, confused at what he saw. A dry, hot wind blew trash along the gutter, making pieces of paper dance in the light of day. Lloyd's dark suit drew the sun's rays like a magnet. His 90 years showed in his face and his stooped shoulders. He felt unwelcome and totally lost in a place he had once called home.

"Where is the theatre?" he wondered, "and Mac's Café?" The bank was still there on the corner. It was a two-story building made of red brick, with a white entrance in need of paint and the same dirty windows. He could still see the words written on the windows in black letters, "National Bank of Murdo". And then the memories of that day so many years ago when three small children sneaked in and locked Mr. Grey Suit in the vault! They had been thankful then for the dirty windows and Lloyd threw his head back and laughed out loud. It felt good to laugh again. He had not laughed since who knows when, since before his love died.

Next to the bank was a small whitewashed wooden building, empty now, but Lloyd could still see in his mind's eye the jewelry laid out in a beautiful array in the window. He and Betty had bought their wedding rings there at Putnam Jewelry.

He crossed over the road, wondering at the forlorn look of the now empty jewelry store. Looking in the window, he saw nothing but boxes, the ceiling was falling down and what had been once shiny glass cases were empty and covered in dust.

Next to that was the drug store shut down now too. Lloyd and Betty always went to the fountain in the back and ordered cherry Cokes. The backbar was beautiful, made of hardwoods and engraved with images of exotic flowers. The stools were high and he and Betty could swing their feet while they drank a coke, sometimes if they had money to spare, a chocolate malt. The drugstore smelled of ink from the magazines, cosmetics and fountain drinks. Now it lay empty. It was all gone.

The town was dead, just like his beautiful Betty. She died not knowing he was there and like Betty, the town was dying a quiet death, slowly, painfully with nary a whimper, not knowing he was there. Murdo didn't know him anymore either and it hurt.

Betty. She had been his life his whole life, but her 85 years had taken their toll. He had been with her until her last breath, but there was a sense of anger in Lloyd, a slow, burning, smoldering anger. He felt deserted, he felt alone, he felt death knocking at his door, but Death was playing games with him and It was winning. Lloyd came back to town because he was going to have the last laugh. If he was going to die, it would be on his terms, where and when he wanted it. He wanted to be home again, to feel the comfort, to see the beauty of the rolling plains, to feel this hot, dry August air, if only for a little while. He wanted to feel life again. What was waiting for him was a dead, decaying place, a place that once heard music on Saturday night and laughter in the café after the movie and the Dr. who lived right on Main Street in a little white house with a picket fence and a tree growing almost against the side. It was all gone. Empty buildings or vacant lots met his gaze and not another living soul walking the sidewalks. Who had the last laugh, he wondered?

He shuffled down the street until he came to an open store. The sign said Gamble's and when he stepped inside the building, he could smell the rubber on the new tires and heard the whir of a fan trying to fend off the heat of the August day.

"May I help you, sir?" a young woman asked. Her voice surprised Lloyd as he wasn't expecting anyone to really be there. He felt like he was the last person to ever step foot on Main Street, the silence assaulted his ears.

"Uh, I'm just kind of looking around. I used to live on a farm near here, maybe you heard of me, Lloyd Bader?" He wanted someone to know him, to remember him.

"No, sir, I don't think I have. She looked at this raggedy, grey-haired man stooped with age and obviously in distress. "Where did you come from? You look tired, did someone bring you to Murdo?" she had a concern for this very elderly man. He looked unkempt, dirty, tired and most of all confused. Where had he come from and where was he going? She pulled up a chair and he sat down with great deliberation as though every movement of his body had to be timed just right. Age was not his friend. He was grateful all of a sudden for that chair. It had been a long day. Only one day? Lloyd couldn't quite remember.

"No, I got here on my own. A nice truck driver gave me a lift and when he got to Kadoka, he let me off. A farmer picked me up and left me here in Murdo on the main street. He sat quietly for a moment. "You haven't heard the name Bader? How about Peterson? That name sounds familiar?" Lloyd was beginning to wonder if he was in the right town. Everyone heard of the Baders.

"Is this Murdo?"

"Where are your friends, sir?" She got him a bottle of water from the cooler and Lloyd realized he was thirsty. It was hot out and he'd walked and hitchhiked a long way to get here. And his bones ached.

Again Lloyd asked if she knew any Petersons around here.

"I have heard that name. I think there are a few over by Okaton but what brings you here? Should I call someone for you?"

"NO, don't call anyone. I'm OK. I just need to rest a bit and thank you for the water."

"When was the last time you ate anything?" Cheryl asked, now becoming really concerned.

"I don't rightly remember, maybe a few days ago but I'm not hungry. Tell me, what's happened to the town? Where is the theatre, the dance hall, the post office, the dime store, the drug store? Where is Doc Gordon's place on Main Street? What's happened to my town?"

Cheryl was now becoming alarmed. It had been a long time since Mac's Cafe was open. It now held old equipment and memories. That was it. The movie theatre had been closed for years also. Murdo catered to the local farmers in the area so there was no need for a dime store or a jewelry store anymore. The bigger cities were not far as the crow flies. Cheryl called the local sheriff.

"Hello, sir, I'm Sheriff John Foley, what brings you to Murdo?" Sheriff Foley was a tall, young, good-looking black man with kind eyes and a worried look on his face.

"Sheriff Foley?" said Lloyd, his eyes lit up at the name. "Are you kin to Thurber Foley?"

"Yes, sir, that's my grandfather. How do you know him?" The sheriff was becoming intrigued now. Cheryl had mentioned that an old man had wandered into the store and he looked hot, tired and confused. Someone was missing this man.

"Did he ever tell you how we saved his folks' farm?"

"You helped save my great grandparents' farm? I heard the story a hundred times. You must be kin to the Petersons?"

"No, sir, my daddy was a Bader, I'm a Bader. Ever hear that name?"

"Mr. Bader, you are my hero, you and Betty Peterson and her folks. I still live on that piece of land you kids saved and Grandpa talks about that all the time. Where are you bound, sir?"

"Here, son, here. I am going to die here, that's why I came home."

"Well, I don't know how you got here, but you need to come with me." That's all Sheriff Foley would say.

Chapter 24

The Reunion

Lloyd thought he was in trouble then when Sheriff Foley put him in the back of his squad car. Lloyd had "escaped" from the nursing home in Rapid City and he knew they would be looking for him.

The sheriff drove along old country roads, over land that was planted with wheat ready for harvest. Lloyd drew in every breath of that country air, the air he had not breathed for more than 60 years. And he loved it, the smell, the hot air, the gently rolling hills that went on and on. Open prairie, his home. He closed his eyes and thought about how he and Betty would ride old Scout over the fields full of wild flowers, how they would fish in the dam, how they would hold hands and, yes, kiss in a moment of pure unadulterated love. He was ready to die now anytime, he was happy.

The sheriff pulled up to a small white house with a large covered porch that wrapped almost all the way around the front of the place. Lloyd knew it instantly.

"This is Thurber's old place! I'd know it anywhere."

"Yep, come on in, Mr. Bader. I have a surprise for you."

Lloyd stepped in to find a small, comfortable home not much different than he remembered it. There was a potbelly stove in the main room, a claw foot dining room table and four chairs. Over by the window was a hospital bed, and on that bed lay Thurber!!!

Lloyd shuffled over to where his longtime friend lay, gazing at the grain as it raised its collective head to heaven.

"Thurber, my old friend, how good it is to see you again." Lloyd couldn't help it, a gazillion years of pain, suffering, fighting for the right to exist, to have a small piece of this prairie brought tears to the old man's eyes. He thought he had forgotten how to cry but seeing his friend, his buddy of so many years ago, brought back everything they had been through together.

Thurber turned to look at Lloyd. "Who are you?" was all he could say. His eyes dull from old age, his hand withered, his hair white as the sheets he lay under.

"Thurber, it's me, Lloyd, remember me?" Please remember me.

"Lloyd? Lloyd Bader? My old friend? Lloyd?" Thurber couldn't believe his eyes either. And then they both laughed, grabbed the others' hand and held as tight as they could and that day at the bank came rushing in like it was yesterday.

"Lloyd, where have you been? What have you been doing all these years? How is Betty?"

"Our Betty is gone, Thurber. She died a few years back. I was with her to the end and she went real quiet like, but I miss my girl. You and I spent years in different places, you here, me out West, Denver but, Thurber, this was always home. Betty would never have kids and I knew that when we married but we had each other and that was enough. We are prairie people, tried and true, always have been. And how about you, Thurber, old friend? Have the years been good to you?"

Thurber looked out the window again and back at his old friend still holding his hand.

"I never left Lloyd. When Mother and Father died here, I took over. You helped save this farm and this is all I've ever known. Thank you, my good friend. I married a Winslow girl and we had four kids, now all grown and moved away. I've had a good life, Lloyd, a real good life thanks in part to that time at the Bank. Now I am going to die and it will be here where I belong. I am at peace. But what about you, Lloyd? What brings you back after so many years gone?"

Lloyd thought for a moment and then said, "I will die here too, Thurber. It's my time and in my heart I never really left. When things were quiet or bad or sad, I came back here to my roots. Always on my mind, you know? But I am so happy I got to say goodbye to you. Who knows, maybe we will see each other again, huh? Maybe we can run again over these fields, maybe Betty will be with us and we will again ride Scout. Who knows?"

"Yep, Lloyd, who knows?" With that, Thurber turned back to the window, silent, shutting out the world but holding tight to Lloyd's hand. They sat that way for a short while and then Sheriff Foley came over.

Sheriff Foley had been watching and invited Lloyd to stay for the night. He actually wanted to make sure the right people knew that Lloyd was here and he planned on calling dispatch in the morning. Lloyd agreed and they had a small meal together. Sheriff Foley was looking for an APB on Lloyd but so far, nothing was coming through. He would keep him until he found out where he belonged.

Chapter 25

Home at Last

The next morning when they awoke, Lloyd was gone. "Where could he have run off to? He must have gone to get some air." John thought. Walking into the living room where Lloyd had spent the night, John noticed that the bedding was folded neatly and placed on the end of the sofa. Lloyd's small suitcase was still there and there was a note which read:

"Thank you so much for letting me come home again. Thank you for letting me say goodbye to the best friend I ever had. We will meet again."

Sheriff John Foley went out to see if he could find the old man, searching with a sinking heart. He didn't know if he had walked off to go back to town or to head over the fields to his old homestead. There were a million ways to go, but it was easy to get lost in this vast, still untamed land. John covered his eyes against the already hot sun and looked for some time, never finding Lloyd. He went back into the house and reported in, letting them know he was looking for a missing man. Over the late night an APB came in about an elderly man who left the nursing home in Rapid City and was missing. Sheriff Foley knew right away who it was. After letting dispatch know he found him, John moved again outside, now really hot with nothing to stop the rays of a summer sun beating down on the prairie. The dogs were barking down by the fishing pond so Sheriff Foley moved in that direction. The pond was starting to dry up, but they had been fortunate to have some rain of late.

He discovered Lloyd there. Lloyd lay face down in the water having been there for awhile. Sheriff Foley pulled his lifeless body to shore and sat contemplating this old man that had lived so much. He called for an ambulance but knew it was far too late to help Lloyd. Had he done this on purpose? Lloyd left a note and it read, "I did it my way." That was all, but Sheriff Foley was sure now. Lloyd came back to his home, his history, his life. He never really left. What was it he said? Oh yeah, he's prairie people, plain and simple. And one more thing Lloyd had written on his note, a date, something Sheriff Foley didn't quite understand. Please, cremate me, spread my ashes on the old homestead and do it on the 13th. The 13th of summer. Thank you.

"What day is it, Sheriff?" asked the attendant as they put Lloyd's body in the ambulance.

"It's the 13th, Roy. The 13th of Summer."

* 9 7 8 9 6 5 5 7 7 9 5 9 2 *